My Stray Cat

A Small-Town Shifter Romance

Shelley Munro

For Paul.

Introduction

I MET A MALE lion shifter in the pub last night. Not that my father would approve since it reinforces my gay status, but Lucas Huntingdon is incredible. Tall. Golden. Sexy. Our gazes met, and we clicked. The evening turned into night. The sex was hot. Intense. Real magic that doesn't happen every day. Hell, it electrified me. By the time the night was over, I craved more...I hungered for a future because it's no fun living alone like a stray cat. I'm just like every Middlemarch shifter, gay or not. All I want is love.

Note: Readers first met Saul Sinclair in *My Scarlet Woman*. He appeared in *My Estranged Lover*, and now he gets his own story in *My Stray Cat*.

Chapter 1

Kicked Out

"SAUL, WHY CAN'T YOU settle like the Mitchell boys? They've found mates. If they can catch a woman, so can you." My father sat at the head of the table, the flat of his hand thumping the tabletop to punctuate his words, laying down the law.

While he was busy lecturing me, I stared at my mother. She stood by the stove, stirring a pot for our dinner, nodding the entire time. Her jaw-length blonde hair swished around her face, confirming she agreed with her life partner. My feline snarled inside my mind as ruffled as his human side. It was as if they joined at the hip, programmed by fate to make the same decisions. Hold the same opinions.

Fine for them.

My fingers closed around the can of beer on the table in front of me while I acknowledged I was a puzzle to my parents. A twenty-five-year-old disappointment. They couldn't work out why I wasn't out chasing skirt, behaving in the same way as the rest of my friends and male shifters of marriageable age.

My father droned on, repeating more of the same. Although my mouth curled in a lazy grin, I was anything but relaxed.

"What about the Matthews girl? I hear she's returning from Dunedin. We'll invite her for dinner," my father said.

I stiffened, my spine hitting the back of my wooden chair. Feline shifters were hardwired to find a mate. It just *was*, and I understood that, but no way was I going to get saddled with someone of my parents' choosing. The old man continued with the lecture, and eventually, I tuned out of his reprimand.

The thing was, I didn't do women. I was into men, and nothing could change that fact. After soul-searching and experimentation, I'd accepted my preferences. I differed from most males, both human and shifter.

There was no mate in my future.

"Damn it, boy." My father smashed his fist into the

table, his face turning red with irritation. The knives and forks and condiments my mother had placed on the table jumped and danced out of place. "Didn't you meet anyone while you were at Glenshee Station? Or while you were traveling? Are you listening?"

I inhaled, wondering how this conversation had slithered into dangerous territory so fast. I blamed my friends Saber, Felix, and Leo Mitchell for putting ideas into the old man's head. A spate of matings had taken place in Middlemarch during the last two years, and my parents were anxious to have grandchildren.

"Yeah, Dad. I hear you. The neighbors can probably hear you." Giving in to the urge to come home to see my parents had been a mistake.

"Listen to your father, son." My mother's voice was low and soothing as if she recognized how close we were to jumping into a shouting match, into saying things we'd regret.

"I'm listening." But it was a lie. I didn't have to since I knew the lecture by heart. Somewhere out there was the woman for me—maybe another shifter if I were lucky. We'd mate and spend the rest of our lives together.

Be happy. No point fighting fate.

On cue, my parents cast each other adoring looks. A snort escaped before I could censor it—a fact that didn't escape my father. But hell, I was so tired of the constant bitching at my lack of success with women. The same old tired litany. The words, oft repeated, ground away at my self-control.

My father drew himself up and glared from beneath bushy brows. "There's a mate for you. All you need to do is find her."

"Dad!" My tone was sharp, demanding he listen. I jumped to my feet, my heart racing as my brain and mouth jumped into gear. "I'm not hooking up with a female since women don't interest me. I'm gay."

For a frozen instant, we stared at each other. Shock hit us equally—my parents suffered from the announcement while I couldn't believe I'd confessed the awful truth.

I was gay and women didn't do it for me.

"That's a good joke, Saul. Nearly had us there." My father's booming laugh echoed inside the steamy kitchen. My work-roughened hands curled into tight fists. He thought I was joking.

My mother's face was pale as she scanned my features. She didn't laugh because something in my expression convinced her I was telling the truth. Her eyes rounded and turned glassy, as if she might cry. Her trembling hand clapped over her open mouth.

I glanced away, unwilling to witness her shocked pain. "I'm not joking, Dad. There won't be any mate for me because I'm gay."

A strained silence throbbed in the kitchen, broken only by the insistent clack of a clock. We stared at each other, the tension palpable.

"I'm sorry. I didn't mean to blurt it out like that." The relationship between me and Dad had never gone smoothly. My mother always told me it was because we were alike. My mouth curled into a wry smile. Not this time.

"You think this is funny? Get out." My father's words were icy cold. Fierce. This wasn't the time to argue that being gay didn't make me any different, that I was still his son.

I turned away, hesitating only when I heard my mother's sob.

"Don't cry, Allison. Saul isn't worth it. He's sick. Abnormal. He is not our son. Go," my father snapped when he noticed I'd stopped by the head of the table.

"Don't bother coming back this time."

Numb, I continued walking, pausing only to grab my wallet and keys off the kitchen counter. I walked outside and climbed into my SUV, then sat motionless in the driver's seat. Sick at heart. Disillusioned. I burrowed my hands through my unruly dark hair and cursed before shoving the keys in the ignition. My father was wrong. I was normal. I was the same as everyone else in Middlemarch.

All I wanted was love.

AORAKI MOUNT COOK NATIONAL Park was a thriving tourist destination. In the winter, it was skiing, while in the summer, the mountains of the Southern Alps were the preserve of trampers along with the tourists wanting to get a closer look at New Zealand's highest mountain peak—Aoraki, the cloud piercer.

O'Hara's, a bar near The Hermitage Hotel in Mount Cook village, was bustling with a mixture of tourists, workers, and locals. Since it was a Saturday night, the bar had employed a band, and a male singer belted out a rock classic. Several couples danced, bodies writhing in time to the beat of the music in the dimly lit room.

I leaned against the bar and observed the customers while sipping my beer. I'd been in the village for two months, working for a company that offered guided walks around the Mount Cook region. The seasonal job suited my love of the outdoors. I enjoyed the mountain air and shifting and running in relative privacy, possible because of the sparseness of the population. I'd be sorry once the job ended in a few weeks. Mount Cook was a shifter's paradise. People surrounded me, yet loneliness sat like a weight on my shoulders.

A woman pushed into a gap at the bar between me and another woman. The new arrival was gorgeous, tall and slender but not too skinny. When she pressed closer, I tensed at her wild scent.

Shifter. The woman was a shifter.

I inhaled her scent with something akin to pleasure because I hadn't seen another shifter since I'd left Middlemarch.

She wasn't black leopard. Not that it mattered because I was so desperate for communication with a like being. Shifters weren't meant to live alone.

And this solitary life didn't suit me.

My gaze wandered across the smooth, tanned skin of her face. She was lovely. I could appreciate her stunning tawny beauty even though I preferred males.

"What are you staring at?" she demanded, catching me off guard. Her brown eyes flashed, and she tossed a luxurious mane of blonde curls over her shoulder. Irritation underlined the move but instead of making me back off, she made me grin.

"You," I drawled. "I'm staring at you." I'm not sure where the urge to tease her came from, but since her attention centered on me, I ran with the impulse.

"Don't bother, pretty boy. You're wasting your time blinking your cute green eyes and flashing your dimples at me. I'm not interested." South Africa colored her voice, the accent strong and brash.

My grin widened to toothy. "Most girls wait until they're asked before assuming. But as it happens, I'm not looking for a woman." I paused, my gaze running across her tawny complexion, her full bottom lip and dipping to peruse her breasts. My gaze lifted again to caress her face. "Now if you had a brother, I might be interested."

Hell, my tongue had turned rebellious. Honesty poured from me in a wave. We gaped at each other, my words hanging between us. I figured even though I spoke the truth, she'd assume I was joking. But instead of laughing, the color bleached from her face, leaving her deathly pale.

I straightened with concern. "Are you okay?"

"I'm fine. I'm meeting someone. Wrong bar." She backed away, colliding with a solid male, a breath of air releasing from her with a soft *oomph*. She whirled, gasped and grabbed the forearm of the man she'd crashed into. "Wrong bar. Let's go." She tried to pull him from the bar but he stood his ground. His blond brows rose while a tiny smile played across his sensual lips.

"Aren't you going to introduce me to your friend?"

"No," the woman snapped without looking at me. "Let's go."

"I've just arrived." He held out his hand and smiled at me. Slow and languid, the sexy up-tilt of his lips played hell with my libido. My heart hammered against my ribs as I placed my hand in his. His fingers tightened around mine. Our gazes caught and held, and it wasn't in the normal, casual way of two males meeting.

It was more. Much more. Direct. A moment of pure honesty, and suddenly I knew why the woman appeared worried.

"I'm Lucas Huntingdon," he said. "This is my sister Leticia."

Sister.

I tightened my grip on Lucas's hand. Just a fraction to let him know I returned his interest before releasing it. "Saul Sinclair."

"Can I buy you a drink, Saul?" Lucas's brown eyes held glints of gold. His blond hair surrounded his head in a halo, a mass of golden curls. I picked up the same hint of shifter on the air and everything clicked into place. South Africa and shifter.

Lion.

Intrigued, I continued to stare. My cock reared against the fly of my jeans, my libido shooting into high gear. Other than one-night stands, I had met no one who interested me for months. There had been Nick, my roommate while I'd attended Otago University for my Bachelor of Science in Dunedin, but we'd parted ways when he'd decided he wanted marriage and children. Traditional. He'd broken my heart, and I hadn't wanted anyone for a long time. After that, I'd had short-term relationships since it was difficult to find prospective partners while living in Middlemarch. Not that I'd met many during my absences from Middlemarch.

I snorted. Hell, I could be honest with myself. One-night stands were as good as it came. I studied Lucas's handsome face, full of acute anticipation. This was a first. I'd never met a gay shifter, let alone made love to one. Lucas made me think of hot and heavy sex. He made me think of more than one night. His obvious magnetism and golden good looks brought a tempting vision of a future. My future. Maybe our future, even though it was early for those thoughts, I could hope. I wiped my palms on my denim-covered thighs and aimed for calm. Desperate and needy might turn him off, especially when he mightn't harbor the same thoughts.

"Thanks. I'll have a Speights Dark." Not bad. I'd sounded casual and calm. Our gazes met again. Suddenly my night was brighter, more interesting and full of possibilities.

Lucas ordered the same for himself and a glass of Chardonnay for his sister. "Why don't you find us a table? Leticia, go with Saul. I'll bring the drinks over."

Leticia glanced at me before turning back to glare at her brother. "But—"

"Leticia, I'm not a child. I know what I'm doing," Lucas

said. "Go." He made a shooing motion with his hands and winked at me.

Right. Okay. My heart pounded a fraction harder. Inhaling, I turned away, trying to control my powerful reaction to the shifter male. He was a few inches taller than me, but we had similar builds—muscular without being bulky, according to my feminine coworkers.

"There's a table over by the wall." I sensed Leticia followed me, heard her rapid breathing, giving away her distress and agitation.

I reached the table and turned, waiting for Leticia to seat herself before I claimed a chair for myself. My mother hadn't raised a savage. I froze when I saw the tears in her expressive brown eyes. "Sweetheart, what's wrong?"

"Please don't do this. Please just go before Lucas comes with the drinks. We don't need this. We've gone through so much." She let out an inelegant hiccup and tears rolled down her cheeks. "Please."

Her plea tugged at my heartstrings but not enough to walk away from the intriguing man whom I suspected was attracted to me as much as I was enticed by him.

We stared at each other, neither willing to yield.

"Stop trying to scare him away, Letty." Lucas's dark and

husky voice dragged a crop of goose bumps across my arms and legs. My jeans and shirt abraded my skin, tugging over sensitive nerve endings and making me squirm. Hot damn. This man was potent and I wanted him. I prayed I hadn't misread the signs. I didn't think so, but there was always a chance.

"But, Lucas, we don't need him." Her voice trembled with pleading. Tears flooded her eyes again, lending them a liquid brilliance that heightened her vulnerable appearance.

Her obvious distress made me curious. I wondered what the deal was with brother and sister. They were lions, a species that stuck together in large prides.

"We could go home," she whispered.

Lucas set the drinks on the table and turned to his sister. "I'm sorry, Letty. It's too late for us to go back. Too late," he repeated.

Unspoken words ricocheted between them. Leticia looked away first, nervous fingers fumbling for her glass of wine. Lucas walked around the table and sat in the seat opposite me.

Uncomfortable with the unspoken nuances, I stared at brother and sister, scanning their faces and the flicker of emotions—tension, anxiety, anguish and defeat. Uneasily, I wondered if I should leave and half stood before Lucas placed his hand on my shoulder and pushed me back into the chair.

"Stay. Your leaving won't help our situation."

Curiosity nipped harder. Unfortunately, politeness bade me to ignore the siblings' squabble and steer the conversation into peaceful waters. My mother's influence yet again. "Are you touring New Zealand?"

The tears spilled over into sobs. Damn, wrong question.

"We're trying to decide whether to settle in Australia or New Zealand," Lucas said. He frowned at his sister, reminding me of the way the Mitchell brothers looked at each other during a family spat. Being an only child, I'd never experienced the emotions and frustrations that came with siblings. Right now, faced with tears, I was heartily glad of the fact.

"Have you spent time in Australia already?" I figured I'd pretend she wasn't crying and the tears might magically disappear.

"We spent a month in Perth. We have relations there." Lucas's words emerged clipped, a little harsh. It was obvious the visit hadn't been a success.

"I come from Middlemarch. It's a country town, an hour from Dunedin."

"But you're here," Lucas said.

"Yes." It was my turn for discomfort. The Mitchell family hadn't cared about my sexual orientation. Leo had whooped when I'd told him and said his younger brothers could do without the competition. Evidently my handsome face attracted lustful glances from the ladies. I grunted out loud, just remembering. He could talk since he was the pretty one. Emily had contacted my mother and arranged to pack my clothes and personal possessions for me. They were storing the gear I didn't need until I settled again. I owed the Mitchell family big time.

A soft chuckle dragged my attention back to the present. Dark eyes twinkled with amusement. My heart stuttered before flowing back into a steady beat. I wanted this man. Badly.

He leaned closer. "You're the first shifter we've met over here." His words were low to avoid any eavesdropping, but I doubted anyone would hear over the music.

"Not that many around. Should I worry about you being a different strain?" A shifter couldn't be too careful when approaching another feline species.

He caught and held my gaze, his lazy humor dropping away. "Not when I'm hoping to be their lover."

Honesty. God, I loved it. I swallowed to rid myself of the sudden lump in my throat. "Good." I glanced at Leticia. Her tears had stopped, but she worried her bottom lip while she listened to our conversation. She didn't seem too surprised. More resigned. I wondered at the history behind their decision to move from South Africa before telling myself it was none of my business. I hated discussing my personal circumstances so I could hardly demand details from them.

Lucas shifted his legs beneath the table, jostling mine. We were both big men, over six feet so there wasn't much space. A breathless sensation rocked through me when I pictured us naked. In my peripheral vision I caught Leticia picking up her glass and taking a sip of wine. Crap. It was fine being honest regarding our desires but we had a bloody chaperone. And there was something else. Might as well blurt it out before things became too heated.

"I'm not interested in a one-night stand. I've done that before and I'm past it. If that's all you can offer, then we should leave it at a drink."

I heard Leticia's gasp but didn't take my eyes off Lucas.

His dark eyes glittered with unreadable emotions. I didn't know him well enough to even guess what he was thinking. He inhaled, his muscular chest swelling beneath the expensive shirt he wore, drawing my attention. "We're here for a week since we're walking, doing some star gazing, and Leticia wanted to try fishing in the mountain streams."

"I'm here for another month before my contract ends." It was difficult getting the words out, keeping my cool. Beneath my skin, my feline stirred uneasily, restlessly. I'd never reacted this fast to another man before. It was disconcerting, this loss of control, the moment heart took over mind.

"And after that?" Lucas asked.

"No firm plans yet." I considered going home for a while. The Mitchell brothers would welcome me even if my parents didn't. The farm was too much for Dad to manage on his own, even though he was too damned stubborn to admit it. I hoped he'd managed to hire help.

"I want to see the whales at Kaikoura," Leticia said, her tone defiant.

"And so you shall, sweetheart. I promised, didn't I?"

Her face softened, and it was obvious brother and sister were close. "Yes," she said. "You did." She glanced at me.

"Should I make myself scarce?"

I had an idea. Normally I drank over at The Dirty Dog with the people I worked with during the day. They were a good crowd, and I liked them, but tonight instinct had led me to O'Hara's. "Why don't we move to another bar? I can introduce you to my friends and coworkers. Two are keen fishermen. They might give you a few hints."

Lucas's smile deepened. "Letty, you can swap fishy stories."

"Exaggerate about catches," I added.

Leticia's full bottom lip pouted. I began to apologize when I noticed a slight quiver. Seconds later she wore a full-out smile. I gaped before Lucas kicked me beneath the table.

"I might start thinking you're interested in my sister," he murmured.

"She's stunning," I said with honesty. "But she's not for me."

Leticia sniffed. "I wouldn't look at you even if you begged."

"Ah." I fought a smirk. "A feisty attitude. My friends will love you."

THE DIRTY DOG WAS just as loud and boisterous as O'Hara's, the words of a Crowded House hit spilling out of the building as we neared. I opened the door for Leticia and Lucas, standing back to let them through. A wave of chatter poured out to greet us.

Lucas paused. "Thanks." My confusion must have shown because he added, "For including Leticia. It means a lot to me." He squeezed my shoulder for an instant. "You won't be sorry. I promise." Lucas walked into the bar, leaving me staring after him.

His words landed like a kick to the gut, in a good kick kind of way. My entire body shuddered while blood rushed to my cock. Tension held me still. I watched Lucas saunter after his sister, saw the immediate interest when both men and women stared at the couple. Damn. The male had me panting after him and we'd done nothing more than exchange a few words, hot glances and a couple of innocent touches. I hoped he wasn't a flirt, leading me on for the hell of it.

I hurried to catch up and directed the pair over to the far end of the bar where my friends always congregated. We found them standing around a leaner, their drinks on top along with several empty glasses. The clack of pool balls sounded when Neil broke for the start of a game. There were groans and a lone cheer from Neil.

"Saul, thought you weren't coming out tonight," my boss Grant said. His quick glance at the spread of the balls on the table held disgust.

"Thought I'd bring my friends to meet you," I said easily. "This is Lucas and his sister Leticia. They're here for the next week." I pointed to my boss and workmates, listing names. "Grant. Neil. Steven. Dave. Gaylene. John. Sue."

The next hour crawled by in slow motion. We had drinks, a game of pool and laughed and teased each other. I was pleased to see Leticia relax, and I noticed a couple of the guys acted interested.

"Are you ready to go?" The heat in Lucas's gaze caused a series of ripples through my body. The hard ache near my chest reminded me it was time to breathe. Breathless. *Again*. This male had the power to hurt me. I sensed it, yet didn't consider walking away or slowing our pace. Neither was an option.

I glanced at Leticia. "Will your sister be okay?"

"Yeah. Thanks to you."

Leticia caught my gaze. My brows rose in a silent question. She glanced at her brother before looking back.

Weird. It was almost as if they were communicating telepathically. Her lips curved in a secret smile, her nod imperceptible before she turned away to survey the pool table and her next shot.

Relief tinged with anticipation flooded through me. I drew a sharp breath, catching the musky scent of shifter along with a hint of pine from Lucas's aftershave. Time to move this show along to the next stage.

We said our goodbyes before walking out into the cool clear night. A blanket of stars twinkled in the sky above while the moon hung high in the sky, casting light over the surrounding mountains. Right now they appeared as dark, hulking shapes, but in the sunlight they were spectacular, a play of purple, gray and blue with a touch of snow at the top. When we paused in the middle of the footpath, a night bird shrieked before falling silent.

"My place or yours?" Lucas asked, touching my arm.

I grasped his callused hand and tugged him deep into the shadows of the pub where no prying eyes could see. With no warning my mouth crushed his. No finesse or gentleness, just truth and desire. Passion. Luckily Lucas didn't protest. He leaned into me, gripping my shoulders tight. Our lips moved together before we both opened our mouths and took the kiss into carnal, tongues sliding together, tastes mingling. His tongue was rough, the coarse abrasiveness shooting pleasure straight to my cock. I ground my hips against him, my eyes closing to savor the zap of friction when our erections rubbed together. This loving would be good. Hard to see anything different when we struck sparks off each other with a mere touch.

I pulled away as suddenly as I'd grabbed Lucas and rested my forehead against his for a scant second before stepping back. "Your place. It will be more private than the hostel where I'm staying."

Chapter 2

Sweet Harmony

Lucas and Leticia were staying at The Hermitage. We strode into the foyer, looking neither left nor right as we headed for the elevator. Lucas stabbed the call button, and we both lifted our heads to check the illuminated numbers showing the floor location. We waited in silence. My mind was on the kiss. I licked my lips, savoring Lucas's lingering taste. I trembled, desperate to strip and move skin against skin, to feel his abrasive tongue sweeping across my flesh.

A soft snarl snared my attention. I turned and saw Lucas watching me.

"Fuck the elevator," he muttered. "We'll take the stairs. It's quicker." He seized my hand and dragged me past a vintage car parked inside the foyer. I had seconds to take in the sculpture of glittering silver fish and the water that poured over the wall before we hit the stairs.

Lucas dropped my hand and took the stairs two at a time. I followed in bemusement, becoming gladder by the second because I had such a great view of his arse and muscular legs as he powered his way to the top. We sprinted up another two flights of stairs, past shops and a casual restaurant before Lucas turned to the right and prowled along a carpeted passage. About halfway along the passage, he stopped to tug a keycard from his pocket. He slid it into the door, waited a second until the green light flashed. I followed him inside and the door shut after me, closing with a muted click.

The room was decked out in shades of cream with dark cream covers on the two queen-size beds. I couldn't remember the exact color shade but had seen it when my mother had dragged me into a furniture store in Dunedin last year.

It was a standard hotel room with a desk and chair against the wall along with the obligatory television and local artwork on the walls. The thing that propelled the room to special and spectacular was the large window that took up most of one wall with views out toward Aoraki Mount Cook. Not that I could see much at the moment.

"Strip," Lucas barked, his hands working on the buttons of his white shirt.

"What about Leticia?" I asked.

"She has her own room."

My brows shot up. "Are you made of money? The room rates here are steep."

Lucas's gaze bore into me. "Yeah, we have money. Is that a problem?"

"It could be," I said. "I'm not rich." And I'd hate the label of moneygrubber.

"So?" Lucas prowled toward me, his expression mean and dangerous. He stopped inches away, his brown eyes glaring golden sparks. "I'm not interested in your money. It's your body I want to fuck, not your bank account. That plain enough?"

"Crystal." I held back a chuckle.

"Hell." Disgust shaded his voice. "I've never met a male who liked to talk so much. Can we continue now?"

"Yeah." I dragged my polo shirt over my head and tossed it aside. With my eyes on Lucas, I undid my jeans. The unveiling of Lucas's body distracted me. Smooth golden skin stretched across magnificent muscles. Unlike me, a small amount of hair dusted his chest, arrowing downward beneath his black jeans. He sat on the corner of one bed to unlace his leather boots.

"Let me," I said. I knelt on the carpeted floor in front of him and drew off the boot. He had big feet. My gaze drifted upward to the huge bulge at his groin, a smile tugging my lips. A big cock to match. Lucky me. I tugged off his sock before massaging his foot. His guttural groan, almost a purr, brought amusement. The man was easy.

I removed his other boot and sock. "Jeans," I suggested, eager to see more skin.

Lucas stood and peeled off jeans and briefs in one swift move. He kicked them aside and stood proudly in front of me. I sat back on my heels, studying his sexy body. His skin was golden all over as if he bathed in the sun on a regular basis. Supple muscles played whenever he moved while his dick jutted out and upward.

"Nice."

"I hope you're gonna do more than look."

Testy. I bit back a smirk. "I could touch," I suggested.

"For God's sake, do it," he snapped. His jaw clenched and his face bore an expression of sensual pain.

"Yeah. Okay. We'll do away with foreplay this time." A fib, of course. I loved the tease and prolonging of the main event. It made the climax so much sweeter.

"*Hallelujah.*"

Smiling, I stood and removed boots, socks and my remaining clothes. Aware Lucas was eyeing my body in the same way I'd checked him out, I paused in a pose. We resembled day and night—one golden and one dark—but otherwise matched in size, and I think, strength.

Deciding Lucas had had enough time for window-shopping, I closed the distance between us and kissed him on the lips. This time was slower. Giving. We explored each other's mouths, letting our bodies bump and jostle together. He tasted of beer, the crisp taste of hops dancing across my tongue. I took the kiss deeper, exploring the inside of his cheek and his abrasive tongue. A shiver rippled through me, my hips jerking in response. I couldn't wait for his tongue to rasp against my skin. Without haste, I pulled away, my breathing hard and choppy.

Lucas wasn't in much better condition. "Hell." The word was a hiss from between his clenched teeth. "Do that again."

"What? This?" I ground against him, our cocks sliding against each other before the swollen heads hit solid flesh.

No need for erection-enhancing drugs in this room.

"Yeah." Lucas seized my hips with his callused hands and held me still while he repeated the move. We both groaned, wet trails of pre-cum glistening on our abdomens. "I'm going to do you," he muttered. "On the bed. Now."

"Who made you boss?" I liked the dominant position best. I might want him, but I refused to let Lucas walk over me just because I wanted to get laid.

Our gazes met. Held. "Fuck," he said, recognizing this could be a problem. "Okay. We'll take turns." He leveled a challenging glare at me. "I'm going first."

"Are you a man of your word?" I refused to concede without promises.

"Yeah." He sighed heavily as if he couldn't believe he'd agreed to my stipulation. "I promise we will take turns."

Good enough. I nodded to communicate my acceptance and on unsteady legs walked toward the nearest bed. I tugged the covers back and fell back on the crisp white sheets, looking up at Lucas. Anticipation crawled through my veins and my stomach did a strong flip. A new relationship was always full of possibilities. I was eager and upbeat even though I knew there was a time limit attached. If anything, the knowledge brought a new sweetness to this unexpected encounter.

Lucas joined me after rifling through a bag in the wardrobe. He slapped a bottle of lube and a fistful of condoms at the top of the bed, mere inches from the pillow where my head rested.

Seconds later, he leaned over me, kissing my lips before trailing kisses over my neck. His teeth nipped at the tender skin before his tongue darted out to smooth the sting. I shuddered at the sensual drag across my skin. The trail of his fingers, duplicating the move of his tongue, wrought the need for more.

"What do you think of that?"

I snorted. Hell, I liked everything. I especially enjoyed the intent expression on his face, the glint in his eyes when he explored my body. "What gave it away?"

"You were damn near purring," Lucas said with smug satisfaction.

"Damn near," I admitted, "but still a smidge away from purring."

Lucas tossed his head, setting his tawny curls bouncing. "That sounded like a challenge."

I shrugged. "Whatever floats your boat."

This time it was his turn to snort. He nipped a pectoral

muscle hard enough to make me jump. When his tongue swept across the spot, my dick reared upward, my balls pulling tight. Air whistled between my teeth. Hell, he was good. Or perhaps I was more desperate than I'd thought. I gave in to my need to touch and ran my hands through his hair. It was softer, silkier, than I'd expected. I also discovered Lucas had big ears. The imperfection was damn cute. Grinning, I kept my thoughts to myself.

Lucas kissed across my rib cage and rimmed my belly button with his tongue. My eyes drifted closed to better savor the sensations thrumming through me, amusement at his ears fading. I heard the distant whirr of the air-conditioning unit and a shout from somewhere outside the room. The mattress moved when Lucas stirred. He shifted lower still, his cheek nudging my cock. His breath feathered across my abdomen. Warm and teasing, promising pleasure.

Impatience grew. Eagerness. A gasp escaped when he gripped my cock with one hand and pumped. My hips levered off the bed, jerking upward instinctively, seeking to maximize the pressure, the sensations. He did it again, then there was nothing. No touch. Just nothing.

My eyes flicked open to see him grinning. "Stop teasing."

Lucas was unapologetic when he glanced up at me. "My first thought was to get my rocks off straightaway, but exploring is good, getting to know what you prefer, what makes you hot." He leaned over, guiding my cock to his mouth. Heat surrounded the tip. Once again, my hips thrust upward, driving my dick deeper into the warm heat. A groan squeezed past my lips while my heart galloped. Pleasure swept through me, firing a deep-seated need inside. My balls pulled tighter still to the edge of pain. It was going to be good.

I knew it.

His tongue swirled across the head of my cock. I felt pressure as he sucked, drawing me deeper into his mouth. I groaned—a deep, dark sound—my hips moving, trying to burrow deeper into the scorching heat of his mouth. He knew what his touch was doing to me. His soft chuckle vibrated along my cock. The action of his lips and tongue pushed me higher. Clawing tension simmered inside. I trembled, every muscle in my body tense while I strove for climax. A tingle started in my balls. Another swish of his talented tongue pushed me higher still. I pushed deep into his mouth, the pressure building until I couldn't hold back for an instant longer. I groaned as semen rushed up my cock, exploding from me in a convulsive contraction. He continued to work me while I luxuriated in the aftershocks.

Finally, I gripped his head, pushing him away. Still panting, I pressed a kiss to his hand. I sucked in a breath before saying, "I guess it's your turn now."

"Please." There was a world of meaning in his face, and in that moment I wanted to give it to him—the world.

"Chuck me the lube," I said, lifting up on to my elbow.

A tinge of red colored his cheeks while arousal glittered in his eyes. I reached out to accept the plastic bottle, taking the time to skim my fingers across his chest. I flicked a flat nipple and heard his sharp intake of breath, saw the flare of his nostrils. The heat of his touch seared my fingers as the lube changed hands.

"I want you," he whispered.

"I know." I sat up properly and flicked the top of the lube open. The bottle wheezed when I squeezed lube onto my palm. "Come here."

Lucas knelt on the bed, moving closer until his knees nudged my hipbone. His cock thrust outward. The tip glistened with pre-cum. I set the bottle aside and rubbed my palms together to disperse the lube. Lucas watched me the whole time, his broad chest rising and falling rapidly, belying his pretense of calmness.

Smiling, I pressed a quick kiss to his lips, tasting myself on his breath. I liked it. The possessiveness inside flooded me with alarm but I ignored it, shoving the emotion away to pull out later when I was alone. Now wasn't the time to worry. It was the time to celebrate, to live. I pressed my hand to the middle of his chest, exerting enough pressure to indicate he should lie back on the mattress. Once he was spread out before me, I licked my lips. When I noticed he was watching, I smacked my lips. "All the better to eat you." I grinned at the startled expression on his face before concentrating on more important things. I gripped his shaft with my right hand, spreading lube while I teased him. He'd had his fun. Now it was my turn.

His cock was longer than mine and not as thick. It felt fiery hot, searing my palm when I slid my hand up and down the shaft. His musky scent rose as arousal grew between us. I swallowed as my hand glided across his swollen flesh.

"God, stop," he pleaded, his chest heaving. "I won't last if you keep doing that." He shoved my hands away from his glistening cock.

My heart pounded. I grabbed a condom and ripped open the foil packaging. A snort escaped. I'd greased his cock when a condom needed to go over the top. Well, damn. I'd have to lube him again. A real hardship.

I rolled the condom on him and waited for Lucas to realize.

"Fuck," he swore softly, but my superior hearing caught the curse.

"Took you long enough," I goaded.

"Hands off," he snapped, batting my hands away from the bottle of lube. "Is it my fault the blood has rushed to our cocks?"

We stared at each other, silence blooming. My bark of laughter broke the tension. "You trying to tell me we can't think and have an erection at the same time?"

"It's what women think," Lucas said. "Letty often informs me of this."

"We know better."

"Yeah." He squeezed lube into his hands and rubbed it over his erection. He squeezed another dollop into the middle of his palm and looked at me, his eyes gleaming. "Your turn."

I moved to the middle of the bed and went up on hands

and knees, the traditional mating position for feline. My heart pounded while my stomach quivered. It wasn't often I allowed myself in the position to be dominated. For the first time I understood the female point of view, the trust involved. If Lucas tried any funny stuff, I'd sock him in the nose. A bloody nose taught respect.

The mattress moved as Lucas shifted behind me. His hand glided across the curve of my buttocks, soothing rather than teasing. Maybe he understood my trepidation.

"Are you sure you want this position?" His words confirmed it.

Yeah, I was sure. Now. "I figure you'll return the compliment." The need that simmered through me flooded over into my voice.

"I haven't done it for anyone for a long time."

"Neither have I," I murmured.

Emotion floated between us even though it was early days. We'd clicked from the first moment we'd looked each other in the eye. I couldn't have explained it if I'd wanted to, but it was there. Between us—the possibility of something more.

Lucas widened my stance, running one hand between my legs when the other delved between my butt cheeks, smearing lube as he explored. The cool liquid was an icy shock on my hot skin. My cock lengthened, enjoyment rocketing the length of my body. His lips nuzzled my arse, the light graze of sharp teeth. His fingers stroked across my entrance, sending nerve endings twitching. The simmering pleasure deepened when he repeated the move.

I bit back a groan as his fingers dipped inside, stretching and working me for his possession. Hell, although I'd experienced this before, enough to know I preferred the dominant position, this felt incredible.

The bottle of lube wheezed again. An instant later cool gel flooded me. Lucas pushed a finger slowly inside, stroking and massaging. Exploring to discover what I liked, how I liked it. I pushed back against his finger, driving the digit deeper. It grazed my prostate, the surge of pleasure forcing a groan from me.

"Like that?" he asked.

"Yes."

Despite my confirmation, he didn't repeat the move. His finger retreated. I glanced over my shoulder to see his look of concentration. This confirmed it wasn't casual for him either. It made me fiercely glad, but hell, I wished he'd hurry. I felt empty. I needed...

More lube. This time he pushed two fingers inside me, moving past the rings of muscle and beyond, stretching me. I breathed, savoring the pleasure of his touch along with the dark edge of pain. Blood pooled in my dick while my sac hardened to almost achy. Lucas made a passing sweep across the sensitive mass, making me suck in my breath. He pushed and retreated, pulling his fingers free. I trembled, knowing what was coming next. Sure enough, the tip of his cock pushed against my entrance. Lucas entered me, allowing me to adjust to the width of his cock and his possession.

He groaned. "Fuck," he muttered. "That is incredible." He pushed deeper, and I groaned too. He was right. It felt freakin' incredible. Lucas pulled mostly out before easing back inside again. He worked deep, in gradual strokes until he filled me. Finally he leaned forward and rested his chest against my back. He kissed the curve of my shoulder, a wet, sloppy kiss. When I protested, he nipped me, laughing and kissing me again—this time in the middle of my back.

Lucas withdrew and slid back inside me. Easily this time. He surged and retreated, setting up a steady rhythm at the perfect angle. The head of his cock brushed my prostate, the sensitive gland sending shards of pleasure darting through me. I wrapped one hand around my cock, attempting to balance despite the increasing rapidity of Lucas's thrusts.

"Let me," he said. He batted my hand away, waiting until I was on all fours again before gripping my cock in his fist. Lucas pressed another moist kiss to my spine while moving again. How he concentrated on thrusting and pumping, I have no idea. Sensations engulfed me, stealing my breath. My heart raced, flames of pleasure burning me up.

Lucas increased the speed of his thrusts yet still kept the moves careful and easy to ensure he didn't hurt me. My arse burned but in a good way. I moaned when he dragged his dick across my gland. I clenched my butt, pulling a dark sound from Lucas. It reverberated through me. Our sweat-sheened bodies clung together. The unbearable friction inside me grew even more. The muscles of my belly jumped and suddenly I was flying. My cock pulsed in jerky contractions, semen shooting over my chest and hitting the sheets.

Lucas gave one more hard thrust before he froze, his harsh sound of animal enjoyment echoing inside the bedroom. He pulsed inside me. We both stilled, savoring the afterglow for long seconds. Then Lucas moved, pulling free from my body. I heard the stretch of latex as he removed the condom and turned, rolling over on my back to look up at my lover. Lucas stood and prowled into the en suite. I heard the running of water before he returned with a damp cloth, cleaning himself with thorough strokes.

His slow, sexy smile smoked my insides. I knew just how he felt—contented, fulfilled and excited.

"Come here," I said, patting the sheet beside me.

He came willingly enough before a grimace distorted his face. "Shit, did you have to give me the wet spot?"

I offered him a sleepy grin. "We can take turns at that too."

Lucas seemed to consider because the lines in his face became more defined. He grinned suddenly. "Sounds fair." He slithered closer, wrapping his arms around me in a loose embrace. We faced each other with a few inches between us. "Shall we seal it with a kiss?"

He was a cuddler. I loved it since I was a closet cuddler too. Instead of answering, I kissed him, unhurried and easy until the buzz through my body ended up in my cock. I glanced toward the floor. Another hard-on. Amazing.

I blinked, not ready to go another round yet. I pressed lazy kisses to his cheeks and eyelids before sucking on his bottom lip. No urgency. Just fun and togetherness. Lucas appeared amenable to the idea, and that pleased me. His hands glided across my shoulders, the curve of my hip and skimmed over my rib cage while his lips tasted, licked and nibbled at my neck, my ears and finally my mouth again. I explored the sensitive column of his throat, grazing my teeth across a pulse point.

"Do that again," he said, not shy about directing me. I wasn't so big-headed that I couldn't take a little advice. I repeated the move, one hand moving across his shoulder before dipping to pinch the flat disk of his nipple into an aroused peak. He made a purring sound and moved even closer. Our lower bodies rubbed together, legs jostling and dicks rearing to attention.

"Suck me off," I suggested.

His dark eyes gleamed. "Greedy."

"I thought I'd do you at the same time." I waited for his decision. My body was loose and relaxed apart from my arse, which throbbed. I didn't think I could take him again, not straightaway, but I wasn't averse to other play.

"What did you have in mind?"

"Stay where you are." I moved so I faced his groin and my feet were at the head of the bed.

"Ah." Lucas blew a stream of warm air over the head of my cock. Hot intent shone in his eyes when I caught his gaze.

"You catch on quick." Despite our casual conversation, tension choked the air without warning. Lucas reached out and caught my cock in his large hand. With a delicate brush of fingers, he stroked my shaft. He locked gazes with me again, his brows rising as if to suggest I was lagging. Couldn't have that.

I curled my hand around his cock and pumped, enough to grab his attention. He watched me lower my head and take the velvet tip into my mouth. His eyes darkened and the tight squeeze of his fingers on my dick told me it wouldn't take much to drive him to the edge. I bathed his tip with saliva while I feathered delicate touches down to the base of his shaft.

Lucas licked the head of my cock before taking me into his mouth and making a humming sound. The sensation spiraled to my balls. I wanted to thrust, but held myself still, knowing it'd be even better if I could hold back. I applied myself to Lucas, my finger brushing the seam between his cock and anus.

Somehow, it turned into a competition to see who'd drive the other crazy first. I figured it didn't hurt and grabbed the silent challenge with both hands. Although we kept the pace leisurely, arousal escalated. I sucked hard and Lucas did the same thing. Intense bursts of heat crawled across my skin as blood crowded into my cock. My head whirled at the sensations, the musky taste of Lucas and the length of him inside my mouth.

A familiar low pressure gathered and hot spurts of cum shot from my cock. I set off a chain reaction since Lucas came a heartbeat later, convulsing in my mouth, semen shooting to the back of my throat. I swallowed, slowing my moves while I gave him the wet rasp of my tongue. Finally, we both relaxed. I pulled away and returned to lie beside Lucas. In silence, we wrapped our arms around each other and cuddled, the stubble on his jaw rubbing against my cheek. I fell asleep with a smile on my lips.

Chapter 3

Surprise Treat

Work took precedence for the next three days. Although tempted to blow off my job and spend the time with Lucas, I didn't. My father's fault this time. He'd stamped the work ethic on my psyche so I continued taking tourists on treks, pointing out the local flora and fauna. My footsteps were light and springy when I led my group of six trekkers into the car park where I'd left our transport back to the village. Finally the end of my work day arrived and my rostered days off had rolled around. Two days off and I was spending them with Lucas.

Lucas was waiting at the office when we pulled up at the curb. Our gazes met for an instant and electricity surged through my body. We'd spent every night together but selfishly I wanted more.

Lucas prowled toward me, his long strides covering the distance rapidly. "You free to go?"

"Just need to drop the keys in the office and sign out."

"I have a surprise." Lucas stepped from foot to foot, his expression diffident.

"Yeah?"

"You need to pack a bag. Leticia wants to spend a couple of days fly-fishing. She's staying at Creel House Bed-and-Breakfast. I've booked us into a lodge near Lake Tekapo village."

Hell, I knew the lodge he meant since there was only the one. It was bloody expensive. Too expensive for me. "I—"

"Don't. Please. I can afford it," Lucas said. "My hotel chain brings in good money."

A hotel chain. Hell. I frowned, wondering exactly how much money Lucas and Leticia possessed. "All right. We'll take my vehicle," I said, my tone brooking no opposition. I wanted to contribute something.

I WOKE THE NEXT morning curled around Lucas. For a moment, I lay there savoring the warmth and intimacy. Only three more days before Lucas and Leticia were heading for Dunedin and then on to Christchurch. Although we'd only known each other for a short time, I didn't want Lucas to leave. I wanted to learn more of Lucas, the things he liked, the foods he disliked and everything else that made him tick. I wanted the intimate details, damn it.

"You awake?" Lucas asked.

"Yes." Wide awake. My erection pulsed against the crack of his butt.

Lucas chuckled, pushing back against me. I kissed his shoulder and ran my fingers through his hair, in no hurry to push things to their natural conclusion. The musky aroma of sex underlay Lucas's natural scent. His chest rose and fell, the air whooshing out in a purr. It made pride swell in me, knowing he was happy and satisfied in my company. Cats didn't purr unless they were contented.

"We can go for a run later," I suggested, keeping it casual. There was nothing I'd enjoy more than seeing Lucas in his feline guise and running together. My feline prickled beneath my skin at the suggestion. "Trek into the Alps, stow our gear and shift so we can run."

Another purr erupted from Lucas. "You know when you don't shift for a while? Your skin itches and edginess sings through your bloodstream." Lucas turned in my arms so we faced each other. "That's me right now. I haven't run since we stayed with the relatives in Perth. Right now, I want it more than anything."

"I can't interest you in a quickie before breakfast?"

Lucas pressed a quick kiss to my lips and danced out of reach when I would have yanked him against my chest. "You've promised me a run. God, I wish Leticia could come too. We weren't sure whether it was safe to run or not." He bounded off the bed, reminding me of a kid, of the Mitchell brothers when we were at school. "When can we go?"

"After we eat." Hell, I sounded like my mother. Part of me wanted to laugh at the incongruity, but the wave of homesickness almost did me in. I missed being out on the farm, being able to change at will and knocking around with the Mitchell clan.

"I'd better dress," Lucas said. A wide grin stretched from one ear to the other, a grin that invited me to share in his delight.

I laughed. "Guess I'd better get out of bed."

An hour passed before we jumped into my SUV and headed for the trailhead. The lodge had given us a packed lunch that we stowed in a daypack along with a few more personal items. I'd trekked in the Mackenzie region before and knew the perfect place to shift.

"We'll have to trek for an hour first," I said.

"A whole hour?" Lucas pouted. "Watch where you're driving," he yelped.

"Don't distract me then." I risked a glance across at him and intercepted a smirk along with another sexy pout. My tongue darted out to moisten my mouth. I dug my teeth into my bottom lip, imagining doing that to Lucas. Although my gaze was on the road, I heard his groan. Payback. I loved it.

I parked the SUV and switched off the ignition. My vehicle was the only one in the car park. Good. I'd hoped that would be the case. "Ready?"

"Oh yeah," Lucas drawled. "Hell, I wish Leticia could have come with us. It'd do her good to shift and run, embrace the feline for a few hours."

Something in his tone hinted at secrets. The need to ask questions simmered, but I refrained. It wasn't my business since our relationship wouldn't move out of casual before they left. The knowledge sent shimmers of pain through me. Maybe I should have left it as a one night, then I wouldn't have this strong reaction. I didn't want Lucas to leave. I shoved aside my sadness, determined to milk the day for every bit of enjoyment. Meeting Lucas had helped me understand what I wanted from the future—a lover exactly like Lucas and a job working the land with other shifters around me. I didn't want to hide anymore.

"We can swing by the bed-and-breakfast where she's staying later this afternoon," I said. "Take her out for a quick run once she's finished fishing."

Lucas's expression displayed shock. "You'd do that?"

"Of course." Again secrets lurked in my lover's eyes, making me wonder why brother and sister had left their pride.

"Thank you." Lucas pulled me into a quick embrace, holding so tight my ribs were in danger of cracking. Our lips met and lingered, rubbing together in a kiss that was an affirmation, a kiss that rocked my foundation. "Wow," Lucas said when we came up to breathe. His erection pressed against my hipbone while he ran his fingers across the stubble on my jaw.

"Hold that thought," I said.

"Aw."

"Willpower, man." The cute pout would lead me astray

if I wasn't careful. I seized the daypack from the rear of the vehicle and locked the SUV. "This way." I wasn't going to push, not when I knew Lucas could distract me with a look.

I started along a narrow dirt track that ran from the far end of the car park. A lone tree stood sentinel to the valley, clinging to the edge of a rocky hill. A breeze ruffled its branches while overhead the morning sun shone with heat. Lucas's footsteps sounded behind me and I forged ahead. We walked through a narrow valley, following the path of a stream making its way to Lake Tekapo. Patches of tussock grass and rock covered the lower slopes of the nearby hills. On the higher peaks, the tussock gave way to sheer rock. In the winter, snow covered the entire area but toward the end of summer, only the highest peaks in the Southern Alps still bore a dirty layer of ice. The sun picked up the colors in the rocks, making the slopes glisten in purple, black and gray.

The path widened and Lucas and I could walk side by side. A relief since I swear Lucas had stared holes through the seat of my shorts. The prickle of sensual heat stalked my body, my erection growing enough that walking became uncomfortable.

"How much farther?" Lucas demanded. A glance confirmed he was in the same state as me.

"We've only just started. Another half an hour at least. See that small hill over there?" I pointed at a hill bearing more tussock than its neighbors. "That's where we're heading."

Lucas scowled, but I noticed his pace increased, betraying his eagerness. I was looking forward to shifting as well but also factored in sex. I suspected it'd be hot with the adrenaline of a shift still swimming through our veins.

We left the main path and crossed the stream, heading for the top of the hill. There was a small sheltered area there with views over the entire valley where we could leave our gear and relax later after our run.

Finally we reached the spot. I shrugged out of my daypack and set it on the ground near the base of a huge granite boulder. I sat to remove my boots and socks and the rest of my clothes.

"Ready?"

"Hell yeah." Eagerness pulsed from him in palpable waves, pulling a grin from me. He vibrated with tension, tossing his clothes willy-nilly on the ground.

I concentrated on my feline shape, pulling the image of

a black panther into my mind. The prickle of the change rippled across my skin, bones shifted and rearranged in a surge of pleasure tinged with pain. I dropped to all fours, grinning in a feline smirk and swished my tail as I recalled another recent shift when I'd been visiting my uncle's station. That time I'd faced a knife-wielding woman and turned her life upside down. Luckily, everything had turned out for the best.

Turning to Lucas, I watched while his change took him. His face contorted in an expression of acute pain while a golden glow emanated from his body. I stared in pure awe as his body stretched and grew into a new shape. He was tawny gold with a muscular, supple body. He padded toward me, his mane moving in the breeze. I tensed, knowing instinctively this was the danger time when cats of two species faced off. In his lion form, Lucas was bigger than me, enough to give him an advantage in a fight.

A fight to the death.

A touch of fear whispered through me but I held my ground. Lucas kept coming. I caught his gaze, possibly not a wise move on my part. He rubbed his head against mine, the long tendrils of mane tickling. I sneezed, making us both jump.

Lucas smirked and prowled close enough to lick my face. He flicked my rump with his long tail and leaped onto the top of a large rock. Throwing back his head, he let out a roar. Loud and powerful, it froze me in place until the final echoes faded.

Bloody fool. I hissed, sharp and angry and growled to make sure Lucas paid attention and realize what he'd done. We'd attract attention if he roared like that again. Lion roars were the loudest in the feline kingdom.

Lucas jumped off the rock, landing next to me. He purred, rubbing against my side. I melted inside. Damned fool. A soft inquiring grunt and a rough nudge brought me back to my senses. I growled low and ambled away, prowling back along the track we'd climbed. When I heard the thud of scampering feet behind, I quickened my pace. The scamper turned to a thunder.

Smirking, I increased my pace until the wind whistled through my coat and the scenery blurred. I ran for the sheer joy of running, savoring the play of muscles and Lucas galloping beside me. I came to a screaming halt, taking him by surprise. He careened past me before he could stop and I jumped him. We rolled and tussled like kittens, our sides still heaving from the run. Puffed and out of breath, we settled into a pile, cuddling into each other.

Lucas licked my face, purring loud as a motor. I allowed it for a while before grunting. Lucas bounded to his feet, tossing his head and sending his mane whipping. He padded a few steps before glancing at me, his whiskers twitching.

Lucas was ready to go back.

I rolled to my feet and coughed a bark of agreement. At a slower pace this time, we trotted toward the private area up on the hill where we'd left our bags. I shifted first, my chest still heaving from the exhilarating run.

"Saul." Lucas's soft voice came from behind me. "Thanks. That was awesome." His hands curled around my shoulders and his breath feathered across my neck. I turned to face him, a pulse firing to life on seeing the heat in his tawny eyes. I touched my lips to his. Our mouths clung before I angled my head and took the kiss deeper. The wet rasp of Lucas's tongue, his potent heat kindled a fire inside me. I stepped closer. Chests touched. Erections brushed together. Tension simmered along with the fire. His hand swept over my back, his callused fingers branding my flesh.

"I want you," I muttered against his mouth.

"Yeah." Lucas turned away and grabbed the pack. He pulled out lube and condoms. I loved a man who prepared. He handed them to me with a slight grin.

Ah, my turn.

I pressed a line of kisses on his spine and massaged his buttocks. After setting the lube and condoms aside, I succumbed to an urge to bite that fine butt. I knelt behind him, sinking my teeth into his muscular arse. Lucas yelped, but I held him and rasped my tongue over the red mark before giving him a smacking kiss. I reached around and grasped his dick in my right hand. A slow pump brought a contented purr.

"You're easy," I said, repeating the move.

His intake of breath was loud. "I trust you to make it good."

Trust. *God*. His words struck like a dagger in the chest. Lucas made me feel needed—wanted—instead of a stray cat forced out in the cold. How the hell was I going to survive when he left?

I pumped his cock again just to hear his sexy purr before giving in to the urgency thrumming through me. I flipped the top off the lube and squeezed a dollop into my hand.

After nudging his legs farther apart, I ran a finger down the crease of his butt and teased his puckered entrance. Lucas purred. God, I loved that sound. It tugged at me deep inside, made me hot. I dipped my lube-coated finger inside, stretching and working him, enjoying each lusty purr my lover made.

Lucas shifted slightly and curled his fist around his cock.

"Wait," I commanded.

"Too slow," he griped.

"You didn't think so when you did the same thing to me last night."

"This about payback?"

I grinned but he couldn't see it. "Nah, it's about pleasure." I wasn't lying exactly. I slid another finger inside and pushed deeper, skimming across his prostate. Lucas hissed and my grin widened.

"I ache," he complained when I kept teasing.

Me too. I drew my fingers out and smacked at Lucas's hand when he tried to gain relief. I grabbed a condom and rolled it on, greased up. "Hands on the rock in front of you," I ordered.

Slowly Lucas obeyed, leaning farther forward to open himself. "Yes, master."

My loud snort rippled between us. No way was he a submissive. That was what made our relationship interesting. We were both stray cats but strong, with the will to survive. I pressed the head of my cock to his entrance and pushed inside, past the rings of muscle. With gentle strokes, I worked my way in, pulling another sexy purr from Lucas. My cock jumped on hearing the sound and in that moment, I knew. During the time we'd known each other I'd tumbled into uncharted territory. I loved him.

Without warning, Lucas froze. "Something's wrong."

"I did nothing." Hell, I'd cut off my tail before I hurt this man. I really did love him.

"Pull out."

Shocked, I pulled back, separating our bodies. My cock protested with a twitch, my balls aching. "What—"

"I've got to go." Lucas fumbled with his clothes and yanked them on with rapid jerks. He sat to pull on his socks and boots, laced them and ran off.

What the fuck? I didn't understand. I tugged off the condom, pulled on clothes and footwear. After packing everything up, I grabbed the pack and sprinted after him.

The journey back to the SUV took half the time.

When I arrived, Lucas was prowling around the SUV in frustration. I chucked him the keys and barely had time to scramble into the passenger seat before he took off in a spray of dirt and gravel. We skidded until the wheels gained purchase and shot from the car park. The drive back to Tekapo village was fast. I kept my eyes closed when we slid around the hairpin bends, especially those with sheer drops on my side. I learned something about Lucas though. The man was a hell of a driver.

Instead of stopping at the lodge where we were staying, Lucas kept going. He drove along a river that fed into Lake Tekapo. I had no idea where the hell he was going and didn't want to ask too many questions while we were driving at high speed. I concentrated on the stony riverbed and hoped like hell he wouldn't try to leave the road and drive on that.

Lucas stomped on the brakes. Thank God, I'd put my seat belt on, otherwise I would have dived through the windscreen.

"What the hell is going on?" I demanded.

Lucas switched off the ignition and leaped out. "Leticia." It was all he said before taking off at a sprint toward the river, and mystified, I followed.

Lucas paused, seemed to scent the air before heading off on a tangent. I pursued as best I could, following Lucas's scent trail as he raced out of sight over the crest of a rounded hill. With no proper track, the footing on the tussock and stony ground was treacherous. It was a wonder he didn't break a leg at the speed he traveled.

When I reached the brow of the hill, I saw him with Leticia. They were near the banks of another small stream. I raced to them, sliding over an area of loose schist. I squatted beside him, gasping for breath, my lungs aching.

"What's wrong? Is she okay?" I had first-aid knowledge. I moved closer, intending to take her pulse. "How the hell did you know?"

Lucas smoothed his hand over her face and turned to me full of anguish. "There's a telepathic thing between us when one of us is in danger. I guess it's because we're littermates. Sometimes we just know what the other is thinking. And no, she's bloody not all right. That bastard gave her FIV and hung her out to dry."

Chapter 4

Truth Bomb

I GAPED AT LUCAS in shock. FIV or feline immunodeficiency virus was the feline version of HIV in humans. But I'd never heard of FIV affecting anyone in the shifter community before.

"You can go if you want. I wouldn't blame you."

"What the fuck are you talking about, man? I'm not leaving you." I shoved him aside and took her pulse. It was slow but not too alarming. I thought she'd recover once we warmed her. "We need to get her back to the lodge. Is she on medication?"

"There isn't any. Not that we can find." Pain threaded his voice. "I guess we'll wait until she recovers and move on."

I scooped Leticia into my arms and stood.

"Why are you carrying her?"

"Because you're knackered," I said. "Come on. Grab her fishing line and bag. Let's get her warm. There's a blanket in the SUV."

Lucas ran beside us, toting her possessions, confusion covering his face. "But aren't you worried you'll catch it?"

I kept walking when Lucas would've taken his sister from me. "From memory, feline AIDS is spread via blood and saliva in bite wounds. She's not conscious, so she's unlikely to bite me. She's had plenty of chances to bite me this week and she hasn't." I increased my pace, and we soon arrived back at the SUV. I climbed into the passenger seat, still cradling Leticia in my arms. Tenderness swam inside me as I glanced at her pale face. The two siblings had wound their way into my heart and there was no way I'd walk away.

At the lodge, I took her to our room while Lucas parked the SUV. To my relief she stirred.

"Into the shower," I said. I stripped off her clothes and turned on the shower, pushing her beneath the water once it had heated to a comfortable temperature. She was beautiful, although the large scar on her shoulder appeared recent. It looked ugly, the edges uneven as if she hadn't received proper medical attention.

"Stop looking at me," she snapped.

"I've told you before I'm more interested in your brother. I want to make sure you don't fall on your shapely backside."

Footsteps behind alerted me to Lucas's presence. "How is she?"

"She's conscious and whining about me looking at her butt. You'd better ring the bed-and-breakfast to let them know she's here," I said, instinctively knowing he needed to feel useful. "You warmer now?"

"Yes," she said.

I flipped off the water and handed her a thick honey-colored towel. "Dry off while I order you soup." Although I worried about her falling, I let her dry herself. She didn't seem comfortable with me being in the room. "Use the robe," I added.

I strode out to the bedroom where Lucas perched on the bed and spoke into the phone.

"Is she going to be okay?" he asked the second he'd hung up.

"I think so. How often does she get sick?"

"Not that often. It presents like a case of the flu. But

she's been under a lot of stress and that makes it worse."

"Ring room service and order chicken or beef soup," I said. "Then you can tell me what happened."

"Want to hear the juicy details?" Leticia asked, overhearing. Bitterness coated both her words and face. "I can show you my medical records."

"Leticia," Lucas chided.

"I'm surprised he hasn't left like Gerald did," she said, hanging her head.

"Gerald Baxter was her fiancé. He belonged to a pride from near Cape Town. Leticia met him at a party and they paired up."

"We had much in common," Leticia said. "We were both lawyers, both shifters. I loved him." Tears glistened in her eyes, making my heart ache for her.

"The male had a secret life." Lucas took over the story. "And his family had a few skeletons in the closet. Several of the males mated with wild lions. Gerald's mother was lion, but she wasn't a shifter. Gerald liked the rough stuff and because of his higher proportion of feline genes he picked up FIV."

"We had a fight," Leticia said. "He was drunk and raped me. He ripped a chunk of skin off my shoulder, passing on the infection."

The bastard. I went to her and pulled her into a loose hug. Anger pulsed through me at the thought of her pain. I pulled away and drew her onto the bed beside Lucas.

"Gerald must have known the truth would come out. He jumped in first, spreading rumors of Leticia having FIV and giving it to him. He called off their engagement, made a big deal about her illness." Lucas jumped to his feet and paced, his steps agitated. "He spread rumors. Our pride...our pride is a conservative one. They were having a hard enough time accepting me but Leticia—"

"They kicked us both out," Leticia snapped. "Our pride forced us to leave. Our relations in Perth refused to have us." She bowed her head, covering her face with her hands. "No one wants us."

Her whisper hung on the air. Lucas cast a frustrated and uncertain glance at me before resuming pacing.

I grabbed the phone and rang an order through for soup. "Get into bed, sweetheart. Keep warm." I tested her forehead. It was warm, but not too hot and her color had returned. Once she was in bed and the soup had arrived, I glanced over at Lucas. He didn't look much better than his sister.

I took the tray from Leticia and helped her settle. "Will you be okay if I take Lucas for a drink?"

She reached out and touched my cheek before tucking her arm under the blankets again. "You're good for him. I haven't seen him so happy for ages. I wish…" she trailed off, a flicker of pain bringing a frown. "Leave me to sleep."

"We won't be away for long. I promise."

Leticia's expression was intense. "Do you keep your promises?"

"Yes, sweetheart," I said, maintaining her gaze. "I keep my promises."

I dragged Lucas off to the bar, even though he protested every step of the way.

"Leticia needs sleep," I said.

"How do you know what my sister needs?" Lucas snapped.

I released his arm and opened the door to the lodge bar. With a shunt, I directed him over to a private table near the window and pushed him into a seat. "I don't, but I care for her. Both of you. I'll get the drinks." I strode over to the bar, taking a deep breath. Lucas hadn't reacted, hadn't even moved a muscle when I said I cared for them both. I sighed heavily, my gut roiling with disappointment. Hell, what had I expected? We'd only known each other for a short time.

I ordered two beers and a plate of chicken sandwiches because we hadn't eaten since breakfast. A wave of homesickness engulfed me. I wished I could talk to Felix and Leo Mitchell. Frowning, I picked up the beers and headed back to the table where Lucas slumped in his chair.

"I'm handing in my notice and going home," I announced, placing a handle of beer in front of him.

"I'm pleased for you," Lucas drawled, South Africa heavy in his tone. "You're lucky you have a home to return to, friends and family."

I sat and leaned back in my chair. "You're coming with me, Lucas. And Leticia," I said before he could reply.

"I—" Lucas broke off, his mouth opening and closing so much he reminded me of a fish.

"Things are slackening at work with the colder weather. They can do without me now. I'm taking you home."

"I DON'T THINK THIS is a good idea," Leticia said from the rear of my SUV. She leaned forward between the seats, worry puckering her brow.

"It will be fine," I said when I turned left. A right turn took us parallel to the railway tracks with the Middlemarch pub on the other side of the road. At least I hoped it'd be all right. I pulled up outside our feline doctor's house.

"I don't want to see a doctor," Leticia protested for what seemed the fiftieth time.

"He might not want to see you either," Lucas said, earning himself a chiding look from me.

I leaned over and kissed him. "Either way, we'll work it out," I said. "Wait here and I'll speak to Gavin. I won't be long." I exited the vehicle, leaving tension behind. In truth, I took tension with me. Even though I knew our shifter doctor Gavin Finley well, I couldn't be sure how he'd react to looking at Leticia as a patient. I picked up the brass knocker and rapped it against the door. The sound on the television lowered and footsteps approached the door. It opened.

"Gavin."

"Saul! How are you?" Gavin's grin was toothy, and I read nothing apart from genuine pleasure at seeing me. "Come inside."

I followed his rangy figure into the lounge, nerves vibrating in the pit of my stomach. My throat and mouth dried without warning. I swallowed, trying to relieve the sensation.

"Beer?"

"Ah, thanks." I sat and at once sprang to my feet again, marching around the lounge while Gavin headed for the kitchen. I prowled between two dark brown leather chairs, stopped to gaze out the window at the neighbor's house before returning to pick up a farming magazine off the coffee table near one chair.

"Here you go." Gavin handed me a beer I didn't want once I'd replaced the magazine. He sank into one of the chairs and tipped his head back to regard me with intense green eyes. "How have you been?"

I set the beer on the coffee table. "Gavin, I'm pleased to see you but I didn't come for a friendly chat. I have two friends waiting for me in my SUV—"

"Bring them inside," Gavin said.

"It's my boyfriend and his sister," I said bluntly.

Gavin didn't even blink. "So?"

"Leticia is FIV positive. She needs to see a doctor."

Gavin straightened, a whistle of air emerging between his front teeth. "Feline AIDS. I've never heard of a shifter getting that before. You sure it's AIDS?"

"So they say. They have medical records."

"The surgery," Gavin said. "I'll meet you there."

"Aren't you worried about catching it?" I asked.

"It spreads by blood and saliva in a bite. She'd have to savage me with her teeth before I caught it," Gavin said.

I nodded, relieved and pleased at his reaction. "One more thing."

Gavin's brows rose in a silent question.

"They're lion shifters, not leopard."

"No problem." Gavin shrugged and brushed his dark hair away from his face. "I'll see them inside."

I curbed the urge to kiss my friend since I didn't want to scare him. Instead, I hurried outside and opened the driver's door. "Gavin said to come inside."

"Are you sure?" Leticia asked.

Lucas didn't move. "Does he know we're not leopard?"

"Yes to both. Come on," I said. "I'll introduce you to Gavin then I need to make a call."

I waited for them to climb out of the SUV before walking up the path to Gavin's surgery. The door opened at my touch. I stood back to let brother and sister enter and closed the door after me. "Gavin, this is Lucas and Leticia." I glanced at Gavin and suppressed a grin. Judging by the dopey smile, Leticia had won him over already. "Can I use the phone while you check out Leticia?"

"What? Oh! Yeah, that's fine." A faint tide of red rose up his neck. "Leticia, can you sit up here please?"

I left them in the surgery and used the phone in Gavin's living quarters. I dialed, my nerves jumping to life yet again while I waited for one of the Mitchells to answer.

"Hello?"

I recognized the sultry tones of Saber's wife Emily straightaway. "Hi, Emily. It's Saul Sinclair. Is Saber there?"

"Sure is," she said. "Where are you? Are you coming home?"

"Emily, please. Can I talk to Saber? It's important." I figured Saber was the best person to talk to since he was a member of the council who made laws and decisions on behalf of the Middlemarch black leopard shifter community.

"Saul, how are you?" Saber's husky voice drifted down the phone line, full of welcome and not a shred of judgment. His attitude gave me confidence.

"I have a problem," I said, deciding it was best to lay out the facts straightaway. "I have two friends with me—a brother and sister. We're at Gavin's surgery at the moment."

"Why?"

"Leticia has feline AIDS."

"Hell. Wait there. I'm coming over now." The phone slammed in my ear.

I pulled a rueful face before setting the phone back in place and heading back to the surgery. "What's the verdict, Doc?"

"I need to do blood work. The results will take a day. Hey, don't look so worried, Leticia," he chided. "I don't see why we can't control your symptoms with a healthy diet and lifestyle. Keep down the stress levels. From what you've told me, stress aggravates the condition."

"Saber is driving over to see us," I said.

"Oh?" Gavin surveyed my expression before checking out Lucas in a similar manner. "Shit's about to hit the fan, huh?"

"Shut up," I muttered. Unfortunately, I thought he might be right.

Saber arrived not long afterward. He walked into the surgery looking much the same as he'd looked a few months ago—happy and contented, despite the current frown.

I stood in front of him, uncertain for once in my life. Saber grabbed me in a bear hug, showing none of my restraint.

He openly checked out Lucas and Leticia, studied their blond hair, sniffed. "Don't see many lions around these parts."

"Lucas Huntingdon," Lucas said, holding out his hand.

"Saber Mitchell." Saber didn't hesitate to shake hands and I let out the breath I'd been holding.

"Leticia Huntingdon," Leticia said, holding out her hand.

Saber shook her hand too. "I understand you have feline AIDS."

"FIV," Gavin said. "Because of her shifter genes I doubt it will advance into full-blown AIDS, but she'll still have to manage her condition. I'll know more once my test results come through, although her medical records are conclusive."

"Are you worried about catching the virus from Leticia?" Saber asked. When I protested, he held up a hand and waited for Gavin to answer.

"She'd need to bite me severely for the virus to take hold of my system. It's unlikely it'd spread, possible but not probable."

Saber nodded. "Humans can't catch FIV?"

"No."

He nodded again and turned to me. "You can stay with us tonight. We have spare rooms. I'll call a council meeting tomorrow morning."

Chapter 5

Partners

Leticia was asleep in the twins' room when Lucas and I went to bed. Emily hadn't batted an eye when I'd introduced Lucas as my boyfriend. Hell, I loved that woman. Saber was a lucky man. Fact was, I was tired of hiding and refused to do it any longer.

"Your friends are amazing," Lucas said. A hint of wistfulness shaded his face, and I drew him into my arms for a quick hug.

"They're brilliant," I agreed, "but I doubt the council will let us stay. My father is a close friend of several of the senior members. His opinion will hold power."

"It doesn't matter." Lucas sighed and moved away from me. "Leticia and I are strong. We will leave and find a place. A haven where we'll both be safe."

Panic hit me then. No way was I letting him walk away that easily. "I love you, Lucas. If you leave, I'm going with you. We can make our own pride, maybe close but not too close to Middlemarch. A place where we can run without fear of discovery by humans."

Lucas's eyes widened. Disbelief. Shock. Joy. I watched the emotions chase across his face an instant before he seized me. "You love me? Are you sure? We haven't known each other long." He looked at me with hope. Excitement. His brown eyes glowed with emotion.

"I'm sure."

"Oh man. Saul. Oh man!" He ground his mouth against mine. It wasn't gentle. It wasn't smooth. But it was honest. His kiss held every bit of the promise I needed.

When we pulled apart, I started stripping. "We could take up where we left off this afternoon. It's still my turn." I grabbed lube and several condoms from his pack. By the time I turned back he was naked, the light from the bedside lamp highlighting his muscular chest and slim hips. I glanced lower and licked my lips. His dick jutted up, making my stomach muscles quiver. "Try not to roar," I suggested. "The neighbors might hear."

I ran my hands over sculpted muscles and smooth skin.

I breathed in his musky scent with the hint of the wild, of the outdoors. Smiling at a sudden purr, I leaned closer to taste his mouth. His lips clung to mine in a gentle kiss, a giving kiss that made my blood run hot. I wrapped my arms around him, holding on tight and savoring being with a man who meant so much to me. I pulled away and stared him straight in the face.

"Do you love me?"

"Hell yeah. I love you, Saul," he added, obviously realizing I needed the words.

Awe and a sensation I'd never experienced before swam through me, a sense of rightness and peace. I pushed Lucas toward the bed and we fell onto the large mattress in a tangle of arms and legs. His cock jabbed into my stomach and I realigned our bodies. We thrust and ground against each, snatching kisses and driving each other to distraction. My balls tightened with each teasing thrust. Joy bubbled inside me. Lucas moaned, and I moved farther down the mattress, taking a teasing swipe across the head of his swollen cock.

"Do that again," he muttered. "Use your tongue."

I swirled my tongue across sensitive skin and sucked, pulling a loud purr from him. Easy. My lover was easy.

I grabbed the lube and squirted a blob onto my palm. His flesh was hot beneath my probing fingers. His large frame shuddered with another purr. Breathing hard myself, I stretched him and grabbed a condom. I rolled it on, added more lube and pushed inside his entrance. This time we were facing, and I had total control. The acceptance and the honesty, the pleasure on his face made my heart thunder. I worked my way inside his tight hole, trembling at the hot, decadent feel of him. Fully seated, I paused. I leaned over and licked his dick slowly and thoroughly as if it were a great delicacy. His large frame shook.

"Saul." My name was a whisper, an affirmation.

I pulled back, shuddering again at the fiery heat and the tight grip of him.

"Yeah, Saul."

I moved faster, stroking a fraction harder, hitting his sweet spot. His eyes squeezed shut, he fisted his cock with his big hand and his body arched. Semen shot from me without warning and I luxuriated in the aftershocks. A groan ripped from my throat. Lucas froze, his cock spurting cum over his right hand and chest, his face screwed up into an expression of almost pain. Gradually we both relaxed. I sensed Lucas's gaze and opened my eyes.

He cupped my face with his left hand. "I love you, Saul. Next time we should make it official. I presume leopards mark mates in the same way lions do? I'd be proud to wear your mark on my shoulder."

"Me too," I whispered, my heart leaping with elation. I'd be a marked man, and I loved the thought.

A broad smile curved across my lips. In that moment I knew I'd never experience loneliness again, no matter what happened tomorrow at the council meeting or in our future. My stray cat label was history. I was part of a couple and I'd *never* do the stray cat strut again.

Epilogue

Lucas

I sat in the garden, enjoying a lazy afternoon with Saul, Leticia, and Emily. The sun shone through the treetops, making dappled shapes on the freshly mown lawn. A bee buzzed around a patch of yellow flowers, and I savored the tranquility of the scene, the scents of grass, and the fragrance of flowers.

Saul's friends were amazing, and they'd embraced Leticia and accepted my relationship with Saul without a blink. Gavin was still overseeing Leticia's treatment, and her health had improved. Such a relief! The wound on her shoulder had healed, leaving a nasty scar, but it no longer bled through her clothes and made her miserable and cranky.

Yeah, there were a few town residents who gossiped when we entered the café or attended organized activities, but I think it was curiosity more than anything else. Saul's parents—they weren't the forgiving type. Their cold reaction tore Saul apart, and I cursed them silently more than once while I held him in my arms, trying to offer comfort.

The Mitchells, though—I'd go to hell and back for any of the family. They never gossiped about us or told anyone Leticia had FIV, and I appreciated their discretion more than I could express.

My family had tossed Leticia and me out of the pride. *Bastards.* I felt the sly grin that curled across my lips. A decision the imbeciles hadn't thought through since I held full control of the hotels and the money that came from them.

I stretched out on the lounger I'd claimed and placed my hands beneath my head, still thinking about my family. Not a shred of guilt surfaced for withholding money from them since I'd worked damn hard to ensure the hotels' success, and it was a business I could continue remotely. I'd handpicked the key personnel who fronted the hotels and trusted them implicitly.

Our Perth relations hadn't behaved any better, but they got a pass because we'd been strangers to them.

The tension and anger I'd held close had receded, and it was thanks to Saul and his friends. That I'd found a mate, and one with such an enormous heart, brought unexpected happiness.

Saber appeared in the garden where Saul, Leticia, Emily, and I were enjoying the late afternoon sun. I lifted my head to witness his faintly disgruntled expression and wondered if we'd outstayed our welcome. Saul and I hadn't discussed our future much, mainly because of Leticia. Gavin was the best person to help her, which meant we stayed in Middlemarch, but I'd started to wonder what we might do next.

"Excellent, you're all here," Saber said and stooped to press a kiss to the top of his mate's head.

"Want a beer?" she asked.

"I'll get one," Saber said. "Anyone want refills?"

"Please." It was a collective vote of approval.

"I'll help," I said, glad of the chance to speak to Saber alone. Saul had told me Saber would tell us if we were in the way, but I wanted to ask him myself. I followed Saber into the kitchen.

"What's on your mind?" he asked, reading me with ease.

"I was wondering if we'd outstayed our welcome. Saul

and I haven't made plans, and Gavin wants to monitor Leticia for a few more weeks."

"We have plenty of room, and you and Saul pull your weight. You've helped me with the stock, and Saul has filled in for Emily so she and I could take time for ourselves." He handed me three bottles of beer. "What is Emily drinking?"

"Wine and a ginger beer for Leticia."

"Right." Saber grabbed the wine bottle and another ginger beer. "I have a favor I want to ask. You might want to leave once you hear the details."

I shrugged, intrigued and curious, and followed Saber back into the garden. The man was only a handful of years older than me, but he had a lot of responsibility, including his work with the Feline council. Saul had told me a nineteen-year-old Saber had taken charge of his younger brothers after their Uncle Herbert had died.

I handed out the beers and waited while Saber grabbed a seat and took his first sip.

"We had a Feline council meeting this afternoon," he began.

"Ah, yes. The bra saga," Emily said with a grin.

"I thought I'd persuaded everyone on the board that

dressing up in these bras was the way to thumb their noses at their grandchildren, but Benjamin, Kenneth, and Sid are balking now that the gala day is almost here."

"Bras?" I asked, uncertain I was hearing right. Men wearing bras?

Even Leticia seemed fascinated, and I took heart from her interest. She struggled through days of depression, which was understandable. But right now, clear curiosity etched into her features.

Saul chuckled. "It's not anything to do with that bra fence, is it? The one that the ladies on the council have issues with?"

"No," Saber said. "Several months ago, we had a meeting for the entire community and asked them to supply details of events they'd like us to organize in the future. Around ten people mentioned a wet T-shirt contest because they knew it would cause a kafuffle. I talked the council members into donning bras in weird shapes as a joke and to show we're good sports. The wretches voted for the idea, and now they're reneging."

"Are you asking us to volunteer to appear in a wet T-shirt competition?" Emily asked. Her lips twitched as if she was trying not to laugh. "I could do that."

Saber growled, the sound distinctly feline and testy, and Emily burst out in laughter.

"That was too easy," she said with a chortle.

"What do you need, Saber?" I asked.

"I wondered if you and Saul would wear the bras Caroline designed for Kenneth and Benjamin. I'll get one of my brothers to wear the last one."

"What about you?" Emily asked, her lips still quirking.

"I have my own," Saber said with a roll of his eyes. "Will you do it? There's no water involved. We're doing a fashion parade."

"Yes," I said without hesitation.

"Yes," Saul confirmed. "It will be fun."

"What else happens at this gala day?" Leticia asked, and she was actually smiling.

"We have running races for the kids. Three-legged races. Sack races. There are stalls and raffles. Egg and spoon races. A nail driving contest. Lots of different food trucks and stalls. A white elephant stall. I'm selling cookies. One of the local authors sells his books. Caroline has a clothing stall, and the local ladies host a tea tent." Emily paused for a breath. "It really is loads of fun and raises money for the community."

"Can I go?" Leticia asked.

"I was hoping to grab you to help on our cookie stall. Ramsay and I intend to bake dozens," Emily said.

I was watching Leticia and took heart from her pleased reaction. There wasn't much I wouldn't do for Emily and Saber because they were so generous in gifting Leticia and me with normality, something we both desperately needed in our lives.

"I'd like that," Leticia said. "Maybe I could help with other things, too."

"Ooh, a volunteer," Emily said. "We're not letting you escape."

Emotion welled in me, and tears filled my vision. Saul noticed and shifted his weight. He placed his hand on my knee, concern in his direct gaze. I gave a minute shake of my head and a watery smile, and his expression softened. The man could read me better than most. He squeezed my knee and sat back again.

I cleared my throat. "When is this gala day? Do we need a dress rehearsal?"

Saber looked sheepish. "This coming weekend. I have the bras here for you to try on."

Emily laughed, and even Leticia grinned.

I glanced at Saul. "Just as well we're mellow from a few beers."

Saul winked at me. "We should have drinks before the parade, too."

"I second that," Saber muttered. "I'm wishing I'd never had this crazy idea."

"Have you arranged for someone to take photos?" Emily asked.

"Photos?" Saul said, exchanging a glance with me. "There'll be evidence?"

"Afraid so," Saber said. "But we're getting sponsors to raise money, so it will be worth the laughter at our expense."

"We're in," I said. "If it raises money for the community, I'll go one better and sponsor the entire event."

"You?" Saber asked, surprise in his voice.

"What he hasn't mentioned is that he is rich and runs a hotel chain in South Africa," Saul said in a dry voice.

I grinned because Saul had a thing about my wealth. He preferred to pay his own way, and it was as endearing as it was reassuring. He loved me for me and didn't give a fig about my money. Just as well he hadn't seen my stock portfolio. That would really make his eyes bug out.

THE GALA DAY DAWNED with the promise of a cloudless blue sky and sunshine. Saber had asked Saul and me to help him mark out the various areas for the sports events and to offer our services as muscle wherever necessary. I lugged boxes of garments for Caroline, who was setting up her dress stall and marked out the lanes for the races the Feline council had organized. It wasn't long before the local residents began to arrive, many toting picnic baskets and blankets.

An air of anticipation fizzled in the town, and I wasn't immune to it. I spotted Leticia helping Ramsay to sell cookies, and she looked so happy and normal I almost cried.

"What's wrong?" Saul asked, my lover attuned to my every mood.

"I haven't seen Leticia smile this wide since long before we left home. People here are so accepting and friendly. Meeting you was the best day of my life."

Saul's worried frown softened, and he reached for my hand. "You've given me a lot in return. We're partners."

"I love you," I said. "I can be a grumpy, surly bastard,

but never forget that I love you. I can't believe I've been blessed with a mate. I never thought…" Emotion choked my throat, and I trailed off.

Saul squeezed my hand, his expression understanding. "We have our future in front of us. I think we should purchase a farm together. Somewhere close to Middlemarch for Leticia to visit Gavin and to be close to our friends, but far enough away so I'm not running into my parents. Maybe Lawrence or one of the towns near the Otago Rail Trail."

"Yes," I said, having thought something similar. We need a place to run in our feline forms and to make a home—one that we hadn't had since we left South Africa. "Maybe near a town where Leticia can get a job. She wants to return to work once she's strong enough."

"Deal," Saul said. "We'll start our search next week."

We wandered past the various stalls, which were now busy with customers. On the football field, Saber and a group of helpers were organizing the kids into age groups.

"I need someone to help the kids at the starting line," Saber said. "And one of you to act as a judge at the finishing line."

Saul and I parted ways, and Saber kept us busy with

the kid's events and helping wherever aid was required. I hadn't enjoyed myself like this for way too long, and I promised myself that Saul and I wouldn't become workaholics. We would visit friends and socialize as well as take time away from our farm when time allowed.

My phone rang, and it was Saber. It was time to prepare for the bra parade. I hightailed it to Emily's café, where Saber and the other volunteers were meeting. Saul arrived minutes after me, a broad grin on his lips.

"Are you ready for this?" he asked.

"No." Nothing less than the truth. I grinned. "We'll probably make fools of ourselves."

"Yup," Saul agreed. "But we're doing it, anyway."

"Yeah."

Caroline had made costumes to go with our bras—plain black cotton trousers for each of us. Saber, Saul, Leo Mitchell, and I had forgone shirts to wear just the bras. The three women—Isabella, who was Leo's wife, plus Valerie and Agnes, two grandmothers from the Feline council—wore close-fitting black tees.

"I've arranged a team of face painters," Saber said. "With our faces painted, I thought we'd look less noticeable. They'll have to guess our identities."

"Good thinking," Agnes said. "I find myself nervous."

Surprise flashed across Saber's face, but he turned away so Agnes couldn't see his reaction.

A knock sounded on the kitchen door.

"That will be the people with the face paint," Saber said.

Half an hour later, I grinned at Saul. Everyone had scary Halloween-type faces. We donned our structured bras.

"Wow," Saul muttered. "Glad I don't have to wear one of these every day."

"I hear you," I whispered, not game to say that aloud. The two elderly ladies were scary enough without their faces painted.

Another knock sounded on the door.

"That's Emily," Saber said. "She'll introduce us."

"We should get a group photo," I said, wanting a reminder of this day. I had a mate I loved and new friends who accepted me and my sister without hesitation.

Saul must've sensed my rising emotions because he moved closer until our shoulders brushed and gave me a gentle smile.

I cleared my throat. "Do you want us to parade in a particular order?"

"Yes," Emily said, consulting her clipboard. "I'll call you

to the stage. All of you look fantastic."

"I feel stupid," Valerie grumbled.

"But your grandchildren would never suspect you'd do this, and you'll have one up on Ben, Sid, and Kenneth because they chickened out at the last minute. That's gotta be worth mileage," Emily said.

I watched Valerie and Agnes visibly brighten. "Blackmail," I suggested.

"You're right, young man," Valerie said with a bright smile. It looked a little weird with her zombie's face, but her eyes sparkled behind her glasses.

"Right, follow me," Emily said. "Felix is organizing the crowd and sparking their enthusiasm."

When we exited the café, I could hear Felix on the speaker system and the roar of the crowd.

"I don't know how I get talked into these capers," Leo grumbled.

"You do it because of brotherly love," Saber said.

"And us?" Saul asked. He looked rather fetching in a pink and red number, with swinging tassels that swished with every step. Mine was more like a structured gold corset with sparkles.

"We accepted this mission because we're grateful to you

and Emily for everything you've done for us," I said. "And it's been fun so far."

"I'll be glad when it's over," Agnes muttered in an undertone. "My bra is so sharp and pointy I might take out someone's eye."

I grinned, my heart light. I didn't care if I made a fool of myself. For me, this was acceptance on a grand scale.

"Hello, everyone," Emily said. "We have a treat for you this afternoon—a special fashion parade. First up is Saul."

Saul stepped through the makeshift curtain, and when I peeked through the gap, I chuckled along with the hoots from the crowd. My man was strutting like a true fashion model, his toothy-painted mouth stretched in a pout.

I'd thought I'd be nervous, but the crowd cheered each of us, and I emulated Saul, prancing down the runway with panache and attitude. I spied Leticia, and she gave me a thumbs-up, along with a broad grin. Her phone was out, and she was taking pictures. No doubt she'd use them in some devious way, but I didn't care. Lightness filled me, and I was positive about the future. Leticia was improving, and I had Saul at my side.

Once we'd all paraded, we stepped on the stage together to take a bow. The crowd clapped and cheered. So many infectious smiling faces.

"You look happy." Saul touched my shoulder and squeezed.

"I am. We might look ridiculous, but this was fun."

"We're making memories," Saul said, and I realized he was right.

"What do you say to a romantic picnic tomorrow? We can make even more memories."

Saul pressed closer and kissed me there on the stage. It was quick but sweet, and my heart thudded. Acceptance and love. I'd never thought I'd find either, but then Saul had walked into my life. I'd never been so happy, and I couldn't wait to make more memories with my remarkable mate.

THANK YOU FOR READING My Stray Cat. I hope you enjoyed Saul and Lucas's story. Please turn the page for a chapter excerpt from Leticia's story, **My Second Chance**.

My Second
Chance

Excerpt

Leticia Huntingdon scrutinized the hair in her brush and knew the FIV or feline immunodeficiency virus was no longer dormant. A healthy feline shifter didn't lose this much hair during the grooming process. Fear, stark and frightening, kicked her in the gut and her legs trembled so much she thought she'd fall if she didn't sit. She sank onto the bed, the tremors speeding to her hands and her legs.

"Damn," she whispered.

A glance at her wristwatch confirmed she had little time before someone thumped on her bedroom door. The last thing she wanted was to socialize at a birthday party, but if she said she'd prefer to stay at home, her brother Lucas and his partner Saul Sinclair would worry. And she didn't want that. They'd both been so good to her—Lucas leaving the pride in South Africa to stay with her, and Saul and his leopard-shifter friends accepting her without hesitation.

Her gaze drifted to the tufts of blonde hair clinging to the black bristles of her brush and this time anger bloomed, hot and consuming. It wasn't fair. Nothing about this was fair. Her ex-lover, who had given her the disease by raping her and ripping open her shoulder, had never faced justice, his position as a lawyer keeping him safe.

His word against hers.

She'd thought she'd discovered a home in Middlemarch, yet the disease, the feline equivalent of HIV in humans, would steal that from her.

No cure.

The two words echoed through her head. Mocking and final. Gavin Finley, the local vet and doctor to the shifters, had told her the prognosis was good, that they might not cure the disease but could manage it. According to him, although she had the disease, the symptoms were mild and only exacerbated by stress. So manage it they had, and pretty well. Thanks to Gavin, her health remained good, apart from the latest sign. Not so good. Gavin had mentioned the symptoms to look for and losing hair sat at the top of the list along with weight loss and difficulty breathing. A harsh sigh whooshed up her throat, burning all the way.

AIDS. Such a little word. Such a big disease.

Tears obscured her excellent vision, making her reflection waver in the mirror.

A tap sounded on her bedroom door. "Leticia, sweetheart. Are you almost ready? We'll arrive late to Saber's party. We still have to drive to Middlemarch." Saul.

Leticia sucked in a deep breath, fighting anxiety and dredging up anger to hide her fear.

"Bite me. Don't you know you always have to wait on women?" she added, dragging the brush through her hair again and forcing humor into her voice despite the terror curling across her face. "Always in a hurry."

"Sweetheart, I'd love to bite you, but I don't want to upset your brother," Saul countered.

Leticia couldn't help the involuntary smirk when she heard a familiar masculine growl in the background. Lucas. It was all a front. Her brother and Saul were crazy about each other. Mates.

Unthinking, she drew the brush through her hair again. Her heart skipped a beat when she saw more loose strands glinting amongst the bristles. Setting it aside, she picked up a comb. It didn't stop the fall of hair. Apprehension lurched through her mind, her recent weight loss taking on a sinister meaning.

How could this happen almost overnight? Dammit, she'd followed Gavin's instructions, eating healthy foods, vegetables even. Cosseting herself and keeping stress to a minimum. True, things were difficult at work, the pressure of a big case making for long days. She'd thought she was coping.

By the time she finished, her long blonde curls appeared tidier and less. Thin. Too thin. A hat. She'd have to wear a hat. She'd get through tonight and after that...

Well, she didn't want to think about that now. Dying at a young age wasn't something she wanted to dwell on tonight. She shoved the thought aside and stood.

Leticia dressed rapidly, rejecting the black trousers she'd intended to wear in favor of a short red skirt. Tonight, she needed to distract, and bright colors and long legs would do the trick. Deftly, she twisted her hair into a loose knot at the back of her neck. A low-cut red-black-and-cream top covered her upper half and hid the scar on her shoulder from public view. With her makeup already done, all she needed to do was add dangling earrings and a jaunty black hat. She slipped her feet into black slides, the heels giving her three extra inches in height. After grabbing a black clutch and looping the long strap over her shoulder, she pasted on a smile to prepare for the best acting job of her life.

"About time," Lucas said when she strolled into their den. He and Saul stood close, and she knew she'd interrupted a romantic moment. Envy washed through her in a wave, followed by self-pity.

Gavin. Every time she saw him she wanted to jump him. They were compatible. Possible mates.

"Are you sure you don't want me to leave?" Leticia aimed for light and teasing. She surprised herself with her acting abilities, but then she'd had plenty of practice, pretending she cared nothing for Gavin Finley, the shifter doctor. "It looked as if you were having a private moment." She arched a brow, letting the ghost of a smile quiver her lips.

Yep, award-winning performance.

"Shut your mouth, brat," her brother drawled, the

familiar South African accent bringing a yearning for home. She was home, she reminded herself. The savannah land of the veld was no longer her habitat.

"She needs to get her own man," Saul said, his green eyes glinting with mischief. "Gavin wants you. Why don't you stop running and let him catch you for a change?"

Lucas nodded agreement, and Leticia had to swallow to force back the building emotion. She would not cry. She would not. "There's no magic between us," she said, once again forcing out the lie without flinching or lowering her gaze.

If things had been different, she might have mated with Gavin by now. After meeting him, she'd realized the feelings she'd had for her ex were a pale imitation. *No.* No matter how much she craved the same closeness Saul and her brother experienced, she refused to put Gavin through the trauma of being with her and unable to bestow the mark. One taste of her blood and she'd pass on the FIV virus. Unthinkable to place Gavin under the same death sentence she struggled with on a daily basis.

When she realized both men still studied her she added, "Besides, I've seen how it is between you and Saul. Why would I settle for anything less? Why would Gavin settle for me when we all know he can't complete the mating process? It would be difficult for both of us because we couldn't have a proper feline relationship."

"She has a point," Saul said.

Any other day Leticia would have snapped back a witty rejoinder, thriving on teasing the two. Not today. She turned for the door.

"Emily said there are other single males attending," Lucas said. "Maybe you'll hit it off with one of them."

"Maybe." Leticia kept her reply noncommittal. Let her brother and Saul think there was hope.

She knew better.

CHARLIE MCKENZIE STEPPED OUTSIDE onto the tiled courtyard in Emily and Saber Mitchell's garden, joining the partygoers who had spilled into the night air. He spotted Gavin Finley over on his left, his heart lurching and his feet heading in that direction almost before he'd decided to give in to his curiosity and the weird attraction he sported for the feline doctor.

Embarrassing. From the moment he'd spotted Gavin a few weeks ago he'd thought of him sexually, the yearning spilling over into explicit dreams that had him waking in a sweat and with a dick hard enough to cause damage. Initially, he'd fought his attraction to Gavin—to no avail. Something compelled him to seek the shifter male, and since Gavin seemed to welcome his company, Charlie had given up his fight. He liked Gavin, and the physical attraction didn't repulse him since he'd experimented in his late teens. Recently, fate had led him to date only women, and in small country town Middlemarch, he'd expected to continue in the same way.

Maybe not.

The shifter community had welcomed him and Laura Adams, the other Middlemarch cop, and he enjoyed the forward thinking of a species some would call beasts. Laura had hooked up with a shifter, so the thought of becoming romantically involved with one didn't perturb him. So far, the feline shifters he'd met were decent, and he was proud to call them friends.

"Charlie," Gavin said, sweeping him into a manly hug before he could speak or avoid the contact.

When their chests touched, Charlie's cock bucked and an electric current surged through his body. A soft groan sounded and, mortified, he realized it came from him.

"Damn," Charlie muttered, realizing this was more serious than he'd thought. He wasn't sure what to do next, where to look. His stomach roiled with nerves and mortification.

Gavin pulled away, his curly black hair falling over his forehead. His green eyes sparkled, crinkles of humor forming at the corners. Gradual heat replaced the amusement. He raised his right hand and brushed his fingers over Charlie's jaw, the rasp a soft sound in the night, barely discernable above the chatter of the other guests. "Good."

Charlie groaned again at the heat in Gavin's eyes, the weight of his fingers now resting on Charlie's shoulder, and moved out of the light into the shadows cast by a large oak. As he hoped, Gavin followed to the private spot.

"You knew?" He shook his head, still unsure of where to look. He ended up scowling at his feet. "That's embarrassing." Perplexed, he glanced at Gavin, apprehension a jumpy sensation hollowing his stomach. "Good?" he demanded, Gavin's words piercing his self-consciousness to make sense.

The dim light screened Gavin's expression, which gave Charlie hope. If he couldn't see Gavin, then the feline wouldn't witness the tinge of color creeping into his cheeks. Memories of an awkward first date came back to haunt him. He'd thought age and experience would get him past discomfort and give him confidence.

Not today. No, right now he possessed the self-assurance of a green kid, panicking about how to kiss without bumping noses.

"It's only embarrassing if I don't return the feelings," Gavin said, his voice a shade huskier than normal. He lifted his hand and stroked his fingers over Charlie's cheek again before letting his arm fall to his side. "And I do, so what are we going to do about it?"

Charlie's body pulled tight, awareness arcing between them, the silence throbbing with possibilities. He cleared his throat. "Damn it, man. Did you have to pick a public place to tell me?"

"I'll be happy to tell you later, in private."

"Are you flirting with me?" Bloody stupid question. The man teased with each sly caress.

"I must be out of practice." Gavin paused a beat. "Yeah, I'm flirting with you. You know how it was between Jonno and Laura?"

"Yes." Charlie stirred, shifting his weight from foot to

foot, recollecting the atmosphere when the two were in the police station together—the way he'd felt like a voyeur. "You mean the mating thing?" He drew in a sharp breath when Gavin's meaning hit him. "You mean we're mates? That's why I've been jumping out of my skin each time I see you?"

"Yeah." No mistaking his tone for anything but satisfied. Gavin glanced over his shoulder. Charlie followed suit and saw no one was watching them. Gavin turned back to him and, after a slow grin, prowled closer, pushing into Charlie's personal space. Disquiet had Charlie edging back until the tree trunk at his back halted his retreat.

"You're not frightened of me?" Gavin whispered, his breath warm on Charlie's face. "I'm a real pussy cat."

Charlie's fingers curved into Gavin's muscular shoulders, neither holding him off nor drawing him closer. "That's reassuring. I've seen Jonno's teeth. I suspect yours are just as sharp."

"All the better to nibble with," Gavin said with a wolfish smirk.

"I suppose I should thank the gods you're not a wolf."

Gavin barked a laugh. "You fancy yourself in Little Red Riding Hood's shoes?"

"Yeah, must have a fetish of some sort." Amusement faded. "Seriously, what does this mean?" Charlie wanted to know even though he admitted deep down what other people thought wouldn't matter a damn. His desire for Gavin held more power than the thought of public condemnation.

He might worry about the speed of the attraction if he hadn't witnessed Jonno and Laura together along with the other feline couples. To hear them tell the story, the attraction was instantaneous and strengthened by sexual contact. It took a strong person to resist. "The mates' thing between men. How does the shifter community view same-sex relationships?"

"About the same as humans. Some think gays are an abomination while others don't mind. I'm hoping Saul Sinclair and Lucas Huntingdon will come tonight. Emily said she invited them. They're mates." A chorus of welcomes had Gavin glancing at the door. "Speak of the devil. Leticia's arrived."

The way Gavin's voice softened had Charlie frowning, glancing at the doorway.

A tall, slender woman stood with Emily and two men. One male looked like many of the locals—tall with dark hair—while the other man was a big blond. But the woman, she stole his breath. She seemed all legs in her short red skirt. Her low-cut blouse showcased a set of stunning breasts without tipping over into obvious and tacky. Her profile promised beauty, but he couldn't tell what color hair she had because she wore a black hat.

"That's them now. Come on. I'll introduce you. Charlie?"

"Yeah?" He couldn't take his eyes off the woman and wondered if she'd come with anybody. Probably. In his experience, men gravitated to women with her eye-candy appeal.

"Charlie?"

Fuck, what was up with him tonight? He'd just admitted his attraction to Gavin. He was genuinely interested in seeing what happened between them, but this woman...this woman drew him too.

Weird. Plain weird.

He couldn't blame it on alcohol because he hadn't had a single drink. Swallowing his unease, he dragged his attention off the stunner to give Gavin his total concentration. He hoped Gavin hadn't noticed his fascination with the new arrival.

Gavin wore an intense expression, a glitter of arousal darkening his eyes. "Don't bother looking at anyone else tonight. You're coming home with me."

"I'm not a pushover." While Charlie liked the idea, he didn't like orders.

"Not what I meant to imply. My bluntness is so you know where I stand. I want you." Gavin squeezed his forearm before stepping away.

And that was what Charlie wanted. His gaze swept over Gavin's face before darting over his upper body. Like the rest of the Middlemarch shifters, he stood over six feet, a couple of inches taller than he did. Muscle packed his body without making him bulky. Yeah, it wouldn't be a hardship being with Gavin. His cock twitched, reiterating the sentiment.

"How long do we have to stay?"

Gavin smirked. "Long enough to meet a few people and act polite. Sing happy birthday to Saber Mitchell. Two hours tops. Come and meet Saul and Lucas. You'll like them."

Charlie followed Gavin back into the house, taking pleasure in watching the other man move. He prowled yet didn't seem to dawdle, his tight buttocks flexing beneath his blue jeans. A man who knew what he wanted from life, and who bore confidence and charm. Oh yeah, Charlie looked forward to the coming night. At least now that he knew the attraction wasn't one-sided.

"Hey, Saul," Gavin said. "Great to see you. Lucas, how are things?"

Charlie bit back a protest when Gavin gave both men a quick hug. It seemed his...mate...liked touching.

Gavin stepped back. "This is Charlie. He's one of the new cops here in Middlemarch. Oh, and you can trust him. He knows about the feline thing."

"You might trust him," Lucas said. "But that doesn't mean we have to."

Charlie had to concentrate to interpret the South African drawl. They were all staring at him, including the woman. A blonde he saw now that she stood a few steps away from him. Nice. He'd always had a thing for blondes.

Charlie turned his attention back to Saul and Lucas. He thrust out his hand. "That's understandable. You don't know me. But for what it's worth, I like living and working in Middlemarch. For the first time, I've found a home, and I don't want to screw with that." He grinned at Gavin. "It's kinda of funny because neither Laura nor I wanted to transfer here and now neither of us wants to leave."

"Who's Laura?" the blonde woman asked.

Also South African, Charlie discovered.

"Laura is Jonno Campbell's mate. Have you met Jonno?" Gavin asked. "He's friends with Leo and Sly, Saber Mitchell's younger brothers. Charlie, this sexy lady is Leticia Huntingdon, Lucas's sister."

Was it his imagination or was there something between Leticia and Gavin? Charlie narrowed his eyes and decided his instincts were right. It was the way they took care not to look directly at each other. He needed to think about this. Damned if he wanted to catch Gavin on the rebound.

"Hi, Leticia," he said. "It's great to meet you. Would you like to dance?"

She accepted the hand he extended to her, and he managed not to flinch at the jolt of sensation that raced up his arm. What the fuck? That was weird. Taking a deep breath, he slipped his arm around her shoulders and urged her toward the makeshift dance floor in the lounge. The strange electrical current raced along his arm and down his body, coming to rest in his dick.

This time he kept his mouth shut and didn't react, either verbal or physically. He needed to talk to Gavin later tonight about this mate shit because color him confused about the entire situation. While he understood the concept, his body was having problems with the application, telling him to make a move on Leticia.

A slow song started just as they arrived on the dance floor. Charlie gritted his teeth and pulled Leticia into a loose embrace, one that wouldn't cause any offense to those watching but still way too close for his liking. Thank goodness the lighting was low in here because his cock was trying to exert a say about the situation.

"You can come closer. I won't bite," Leticia said with clear amusement.

"What the hell is it with you felines and biting," Charlie snapped. "That's the second time someone has threatened to bite me tonight."

She tipped back her face, and he glimpsed interest in her brown eyes. "Do tell."

"Not likely." He surrendered to his instincts, drawing her closer. It wasn't as if there was a heap of room for dancing. Charlie caught the humor on her face again.

"Something wrong?"

"Are you busy at work?"

Huh? "No more than usual. Why?" Charlie's brows rose

in a subtle highlight to his question.

"Because judging by the state of you, you're not seeing much action. I wondered if you were all work and no play." Her downward glance left him in no doubt as to her meaning. In fact, his skin prickled, her gaze lighting a path down his body that led straight to his cock. Blood swished through his veins, pouring in the same direction until he swayed, lightheaded and off balance. Not how a tough cop should act in public.

"That's not polite," he said, fighting to keep his voice even. Not so easy with his ultra-awareness of the woman in his arms and his rampant reaction.

"What? I'm meant to pretend I'm comfortable with that spike digging into me?"

"We don't have to dance together," Charlie said, irritated now rather than embarrassed. With the high heels she wore, Leticia stood nose to nose with him. His gaze dipped a fraction. Mouth to mouth. When he caught himself leaning in, he knew he needed a distraction. "What do you do for a job?"

"I'm a lawyer," she said. "I work part-time at a law firm in Alexandra."

"A lawyer. That explains a lot."

"Oh no. He's gonna start on blonde lawyer jokes." The gentle wit made him shake his head. A woman with a sense of humor. Just the sort he liked. "And you're a cop. We could get a lot of mileage out of that," she added.

DOES CHARLIE GO HOME with Gavin, or does he stay with Leticia? Learn what happens next in My Second Chance, available in print and e-book formats from your favorite online retailer.

About Author

USA Today bestselling author Shelley Munro lives in Auckland, the City of Sails, with her husband and a cheeky Jack Russell/mystery breed dog.

Typical New Zealanders, Shelley and her husband left home for their big OE soon after they married (translation of New Zealand speak - big overseas experience). A twelve-month-long adventure lengthened to six years of roaming the world. Enduring memories include being almost sat on by a mountain gorilla in Rwanda, lazing on white sandy beaches in India, whale watching in Alaska, searching for leprechauns in Ireland, and dealing with ghosts in an English pub.

While travel is still a big attraction, these days Shelley is most likely found in front of her computer following another love - that of writing stories of contemporary and paranormal romance and adventure. Other interests include watching rugby (strictly for research purposes), cycling, playing croquet and the ukelele, and curling up with an enjoyable book.

Visit Shelley at her Website
www.shelleymunro.com

Join Shelley's Newsletter
www.shelleymunro.com/newsletter

Also By Shelley

Paranormal

Middlemarch Shifters

My Scarlet Woman

My Younger Lover

My Peeping Tom

My Assassin

My Estranged Lover

My Feline Protector

My Determined Suitor

My Cat Burglar

My Stray Cat

My Second Chance

My Plan B

My Cat Nap

My Romantic Tangle

My Blue Lady

My Twin Trouble

My Precious Gift

Middlemarch Gathering

My Highland Mate

My Highland Fling

My Elusive Mate

Middlemarch Capture

Snared by Saber

Favored by Felix

Lost with Leo

Spellbound with Sly

Journey with Joe

Star-Crossed with Scarlett

9 781991 063120